CRINKUM CRANKUM

ROBERT ERINGER

enigma books

Silver Spring, Maryland

This is a work of imagination. In the few cases where
actual names are used, the related characters, incidents
and dialog are entirely fictional and are not intended to
depict any real people or events.

Published by:

Enigma Books
An Imprint of Bartleby Press
11141 Georgia Avenue
Silver Spring, MD 20902

Library of Congress Cataloging-in-Publication Data

Eringer, Robert.
    Crinkum, crankum : a novel / by Robert Eringer.
        p.   cm.
    ISBN 0-910155-35-6
    I. Title
    PS3555.R48C75   1997
    813'.54--dc21   97-33128
                                                                    CIP

1

The swarthy young man sat behind the wheel of a white Buick Skylark on 10th street, opposite Ford's Theatre. He checked his wristwatch for the fifth time in as many minutes. Seven twenty-five a.m. He looked into his rear-view mirror to check traffic, taking the opportunity to flick a thick lock of black hair from his eyes. He regarded his thick moustache and beard, and adjusted his new Ray-ban aviator sunglasses.

Looking straight ahead, the swarthy young man used his right arm to unzip a vinyl holdall on the seat next to him. From it, he pulled a Skorpion VZ 61— a 20-inch Czechoslovakian machine pistol capable of firing 840 rounds within 60 seconds. One minute or less was all the time he had allocated himself for the mission at hand.

Placing the lightweight, 4.4 pound silencer-equipped weapon onto his lap, the young man reached into the holdall for six magazine clips—metal, slightly curved—and laid them side by side on the passenger seat. He pushed the holdall to the floor, reached outward and manually unwound the passenger window.

The swarthy young man checked his watch yet again: 7:30. He tried to swallow, but his throat was too parched to muster any saliva. He took a last peek at the mirror and swung the car into the street as the red light at the intersection before him turned green.

Au Bon Pain was, as usual, packed with early morning coffee drinkers. Seven to eight was this cafe's very busiest hour, when it catered almost exclusively to office workers from across 10th street. The brightly-colored coffee shop sat in stark contrast to the austere J. Edgar Hoover Building, which towered over it.

Inside the cafe, FBI unit chiefs informally held court with special agents and secretaries and lab technicians over caffe latte and chocolate croissants.

Nobody paid any attention to the white Buick that double-parked outside Au Bon Pain's large plate-glass windows.

Inside his vehicle, the swarthy young man inhaled deeply and recited a short prayer. In a quick, jerky movement, he whipped the Skorpion from his lap, aimed it out of the open window and lightly squeezed the trigger. Seconds later, magazine spent, he swapped it for another, oblivious to the pandemonium his movements were creating, his mind focused only on the mechanics of exchanging spent magazine for full clip. Five cartridges and 30 seconds later, the young man was finished. He planted his foot heavily on the gas pedal and screeched around the corner onto Pennsylvania Avenue, not bothering to look, even once, at the carnage behind him.

One hundred and twenty rounds had ripped the small cafe, and those inside of it, to shreds. The plate glass windows were shattered, its shards as lethal as the Skorpion's .9 mm bullets. Dead and wounded lay in a flash flood of blood and coffee and foamy milk.

A big brawny special agent, first on the scene from across the street, recognized the decapitated head of a forensic technician—and promptly upchucked at the realization that he, too, would have been among his fallen colleagues had fate not detained him with a phone call in his office.

On the sidewalks of 10th Street, life was briefly suspended, passersby frozen in time as the full magnitude of what they had witnessed took a minute or more to register.

And then a cacophony of sirens.

The DC police responded quicker than usual, but their authority on the crime scene was almost immediately usurped by the Federal Bureau of Investigation. Director Bryant Westgate personally took charge.

Westgate had been in his office, signing directives, when his secretary, Cheryl, burst in, pale and shaken, with news of the attack. Westgate was one of the first on the scene, and it took all his strength to refrain from weeping openly. In less than one minute, so very many lives had been ruined.

For over a year, Westgate had fruitlessly pursued a bigger slice of the budgetary pie from Congress to counter the threat of domestic terrorism. This was his bitter vindication—a massacre on his own doorstep. The media would make a feast of him.

Numb and empty, having purged the contents of his stomach in his private bathroom, Director Westgate phoned the President of the United States to personally brief him. Then he ordered Cheryl to assemble his deputy and assistant directors for a nine a.m. crisis meeting.

The swarthy young man was calm as he zoomed down Pennsylvania Avenue. The anxiety he felt earlier had climaxed with the release of lethal projectiles. Now he felt only relief—and an adrenalin rush. The young man turned south on 15th Street, around the Washington Monument to Memorial Bridge. At this hour, traffic was incoming—and light, it being July— so he enjoyed easy passage out of the District, onto the George Washington Memorial Parkway in Virginia. Minutes later, he veered right at the National Airport exit. He had practiced this route each of the last three previous mornings.

The swarthy young man drew a car-park ticket at the long-term lot and drove to a far corner. He jumped out, retrieved his holdall from the front seat and stowed it in the trunk. He locked the car, pocketed his keys and strode to the US Air Terminal. The young man was now clean shaven. The fake moustache and beard lay somewhere along the parkway, not far from a broken pair of aviator sunglasses. He now sported round, wire-rim eyeglasses.

Inside the terminal, the swarthy young man bought a ticket to Boston. This eight a.m. flight was boarding its final passengers. The young man ascended the escalator, perused a magazine stand, then took an elevator down. He stepped out of the building and jumped into a taxi.

"Union Station," he commanded.

The taxi driver chose Pennsylvania Avenue as his most direct route, not knowing it would not be the fastest this day. The swarthy young man looked out of the window impassively as the cab slowly tooled past 10th street, now sealed off to the public, 45 minutes after the young man had first visited the scene.

Inside Washington's landmark train station, the swarthy young man purchased a ticket for the nine o'clock Amtrak Metroliner. He boarded the train with a minute to spare, entered the club cabin and reclined comfortably in his seat. He closed his eyes to meditate. Within minutes, the train was click-clacking through the Maryland suburbs, then the countryside, picking up speed for the two-hour, fifty-seven minute ride to New York City.

FBI Director Bryant Westgate took a phone call as his top officials seated themselves in his expansive, oak-paneled office.

"I don't care!" Westgate bellowed into the phone at his public affairs chief. "The media will have to wait till I'm good and ready to make a statement!" He thumped the phone into its cradle and looked sternly at his guests, quiet, still shaken. "Anything yet?"

"We've traced the car." This was Ray Crandall, assistant director for criminal investigations.

"Go on."

"An eyewitness got a tag. It belongs to a homeowner in Bethesda—reported stolen to Montgomery County police at 7:48 this morning. We're sending agents to check it out."

"That's all?"

"We've sent units to all three area airports and Union station, and we're checking public car parks."

"Goddamit, we need more than that—every minute counts!" Westgate banged his table. "Were there any advance warnings, threats? Jim?"

Jim Thompson, assistant director for national security, shook his head. "Nothing."

"Nothing?"

"Nothing specific. It could be an Islamic terrorist

group—the shooter was dark, Arabic looking. It could be the Colombian drug cartels—they've been threatening for a long time to bring their drug war to us. A militia maybe. Maybe it was a lone psycho with a grudge against the Bureau, like that Pakistani out at CIA a few years ago . . ."

Ray Crandall's deputy burst into the office and cut Thompson off. "I'm sorry to interrupt—we found the car!"

"Where?" snapped Director Westgate.

"National. In a car park."

"Get a forensics team out there immediately!"

"They're already on their way."

The swarthy young man rose to stretch his legs as the Metroliner trembled and slowed for its final approach into Penn Station. The young man looked up and down the subterranean platform and disembarked. He climbed the stairs, strolled through the station and ascended to Seventh Avenue. At this hour—just past eleven—taxis were plentiful. The young man jumped into a yellow cab.

"Kennedy Airport," he grunted.

The cabbie smiled appreciatively, content with landing a big fare. He aimed his badly-suspended vehicle across town to the FDR Expressway.

On the cab's radio, WCBS reported live from Washington on an attack hours earlier at a coffee shop known to be an FBI hangout.

"We can now confirm 12 dead and 26 wounded, nine critically," announced a reporter on the scene. "Casualties have been taken to George Washington and Georgetown hospitals and there is a call for volunteers willing to give blood. Most of the victims worked at FBI headquarters across the street. It is believed that one or two attackers fired from a moving car. We are told that no arrests have been made. The FBI has announced a news conference at four p.m. WCBS will bring it to you live."

The swarthy young man listened with nonchalance. Four p.m. By that hour he would be far, far away. He would have liked to hear more, but the cabbie switched to Rush Limbaugh.

Approaching JFK 35 minutes later, the cabbie looked back for additional guidance.

"Air France."

It took another eight minutes to reach one of JFK's oldest terminals, reserved for foreign airlines that did not possess gateways of their own.

The swarthy young man pushed a fifty-dollar bill through a cash slot in the dirty window partition. "Keep the change." He alighted from the vehicle, strode into the terminal and bought himself a ticket for the French carrier's next flight out.

FBI Director Westgate was on the phone with the attorney general, vacationing in California, when the division chief, counter-terrorism, burst into the director's office to consult in whispers with his superior, Jim Thompson.

Thompson thanked the man and dismissed him. "We're doing everything we can, sir. Yes. Yes, I know. No. It's not necessary. I'll keep you informed." Westgate put down the phone and wiped his brow. The building's air conditioner was not keeping pace with the relentless summer heat.

"We have prints," announced Thompson. "And a weapon. They're bringing everything in."

Bryant picked up another shrill phone and listened. "Dear, God." he said. "Two more criticals have died. One of them, James Bishop."

Thompson shook his head, closed his eyes. Bishop, an ASAC—special-agent-in-charge—had been running an extremely sensitive foreign counter-intelligence operation. Had Bishop been the target? This thought crossed Thompson's mind, but he kept it to himself.

The swarthy young man smiled at an attractive female flight attendant, boarded the sleek plane and settled into his seat. He took a long look at the Manhattan skyline as the aircraft rocketed down the runway, circled, and aimed itself in a northwesterly direction over the Atlantic Ocean.

"We have a name!" Ray Crandall burst into Director Westgate's office, which had, through the long day, doubled as a crisis center.

"Something's up, I'll call you back." Westgate slammed the phone into its cradle and looked up.

"Ahmed Matsalah."

"An Arab . . ?"

"A Kurd."

"From where?" Director Westgate knew that Kurdistan was actually divided by three countries, which all hated Kurds, who, divided into tribes, hated each other.

"An Iraqi Kurd."

"What was he doing here?" Westgate scowled.

"He came in on a student visa for a graduate program at American University. We have an address for him near AU. I've sent four agents."

Crandall passed a document across Westgate's desk. The director studied the two-year-old photograph of Matsalah. That's how long the 26 year-old Kurd had been in the United States, according to his visa.

Westgate glanced at the big round clock on his office wall: 3:37.

"Fax this picture to police stations nationwide. And airports—every international airport in the country. And all border crossings! Immediately!"

Westgate was on his feet, pacing in shirtsleeves.

"Do we use this name and picture at the news conference?" This was the harassed public affairs chief, who had thus far evaded phone calls from every news weekly and big city paper in the country.

"No. All we're saying is that we're on the trail of a suspect. Don't name him."

"Got it."

"I'm going to make a statement myself," said Westgate. The director had cultivated a take-charge approach from his first day on the job six years before. He wasn't one to hide behind his desk. Westgate steadied his gaze on Ray Crandall. "Contact every airline in the country. See if this Kurd has flight plans. We don't have much time." Westgate retrieved his suit jacket from a hanger and adjourned to his private bathroom to groom himself for the cameras.

"This is a very sad day for the FBI." Westgate began his statement, light bulbs popping, video cameras trained on his drawn, pale but composed countenance. "You all know what happened early this morning, at a coffee shop opposite our headquarters. I can confirm that 14 persons are dead. Eleven of them were employees of the Bureau. Our deepest sympathy goes out to the families of these victims in their time of grief. We will not release names until we are certain all next of kin have been informed. Our investigation into this tragedy has begun. We shall pursue the killer or killers wherever they may hide. We will make additional information available to you in due course."

"Was this a terrorist attack?"

The media had been told that the director would

not answer questions, but this did not deter Scott Robinson, CBS News's up-and-coming pretty boy.

"We're studying all possibilities," said Westgate. "Thank you."

Other reporters, inspired by Robinson, began to shout questions of their own as Westgate left the podium, replaced by his public affairs chief, who tried to regain order.

The director's personal aide whispered an urgent message into Westgate's ear: Matsalah, the Kurdish suspect, had flown to Boston.

"What time?" demanded Westgate.

"An eight a.m. flight on US Air. It arrived at 9:20."

"Focus on Logan," snapped the director. "Tonight's flights to Europe. And freight ships. And the Canadian border."

Westgate rushed back to his office.

"We have more news," Crandall greeted him.

"I just heard. Boston."

"No. He bought a ticket to Boston, but never got on the plane. He's in the air now."

"Going where?"

"Paris."

"At this time of day?" Westgate checked his watch irritably. It was his experience that flights to Europe left in the evening.

"He's on the Concorde. Air France. It left JFK at one p.m."

"Concorde? That doesn't sound like a student's budget to me."

"No, it doesn't. One way is almost four grand. Matsalah paid cash."

"How long does Concorde take to Paris?"

"Three hours, forty minutes."

Westgate checked his watch again. "Holy Catfish! He's going to land in 15 minutes! Have you contacted the French?"

"We have somebody on it right now."

"And our embassy?"

"We're trying to locate the ambassador. She's at a dinner party."

"Get somebody to the airport in case the French screw up. Call our legat at home!"

"We did. She's on her way to Charles De Gaulle."

Ahmed Matsalah sipped black Columbian coffee as Flight 001 descended subsonically in the purply summer night sky over Paris. He fumbled with his Swatch wristwatch and set it six hours forward to 10:30. This was the way to do the Atlantic, he mused, full and content after feasting on caviar, crab claws and filet mignon.

The jet thumped the ground. Matsalah stood up, smiled at the flight attendant and disembarked.

Four French police cars screeched to a halt in front of Terminal 2A. A dozen uniformed and plainclothes officers jumped from their vehicles and raced into the terminal building, quiet and deserted at this late hour, except for the last few Concorde passengers clearing Customs.

The police converged on the Air France information desk, on Immigration and Customs—on anyone still on duty—and when they realized they had probably missed the man for whom they'd been dispatched, they raced back and forth across the terminal floor, checking toilets and bus-stops and dark corners.

If Ahmed Matsalah were still around, he had made himself invisible.

Six minutes before their arrival, Matsalah had climbed into a taxi. On his way out of Roissy, toward central Paris, his vehicle narrowly missed colliding with a Renault 10. Its driver, Sally Pippin, the FBI's Paris-based legat, sped to join the police at Terminal 2A.

"He's gone!" Sally Pippin shouted into her cell phone. She stood alone in the near-empty terminal building as gendarmes continued their fruitless scramble.

These words flew out of Westgate's phone, on loudspeaker, for his assembled officials to hear.

Director Westgate gasped, then thumped his right fist onto his desk with great force. "Goddam French— they've screwed us again!"

"Hello? Hello?" Sally Pippin had never spoken directly to the director of the FBI. "What do you want me to do?"

"Go find the top-ranking Immigration official and tell him I'm going to get the President of the United States to shove the Eiffel Tower up his ass!"

Bryant Westgate was still fuming at six p.m. He knew from experience that once a suspect crossed into a foreign country, even a friendly one, jurisdiction problems hampered an investigation. Apprehension was almost impossible—and that was if you could *find* your suspect.

Secretaries worked feverishly around the director to rearrange his calendar, which had been turned topsy-turvy with funeral arrangements across the country.

The ringing of Westgate's personal fax machine just behind him went unnoticed amid the clanging of other phones. The transmission was complete before it caught Westgate's eye. He ripped it from the machine, propped a pair of reading glasses upon his nose and read:

Communique # 1

We desire for you to wire $500 million US to UBS Bank Account number 615.305.45J in Zurich.

If you do not, the events of this morning
will be the first of a multi-course meal.

Send these funds today and save yourself
bloodied hands tomorrow.

Skorpion

Bryant read the fax a second time. He raised it
above his head. "Jim, look at this."

Jim Thompson read the message.

"You think it's genuine?" asked Westgate.

Thompson handed the fax to Ray Crandall and
turned to Westgate. "It probably is. No one outside
the Bureau knows the weapon was a Skorpion."

"Half a billion dollars?" Westgate shook his head.
"Do they really think we would pay that kind of
ransom against the threat of future violence? And
where is this money going, the Kurds?"

"I've asked for a briefing on the Kurds," said
Thompson. "Somebody from the Agency will be here
any minute."

"The Agency?" sneered Westgate. "Cancel it! I
don't want the Agency involved. Call NSC or State."

Thompson nodded, picked up the phone, said a
few words. "Done." He paused. "I'd like to call
Dalkin."

"Jeff Dalkin?" said Westgate. "He doesn't work
here anymore."

"No. But we can get him on contract."

"Dalkin has a disability, doesn't he?" asked Crandall.

"Yes." Thompson nodded. "Tourette's syndrome. That's the reason he went private."

"I don't know," said Westgate. "I don't like going outside the Bureau. And Dalkin—he's something of a wild card, isn't he."

"Yes," said Thompson. "A wild card."

2

J ack Hudson was not expecting his doorbell to ring at 6:30 in the evening. He had just sat down to dinner with his family after a long day at the office.

The aroma of roasted chicken filled his nostrils as he walked from the dining room to the living room of his four-bedroom colonial and opened the front door.

"IRS!" One man flashed a badge; another put one of his size-nine rubber-soled wingtips over the threshold, wedging it into the door. Behind the two men stood a uniformed police officer, his cruiser parked in the driveway behind Hudson's Toyota Camry. A large, unmarked van was parked at the curb, near the footpath to Hudson's Little Silver, New Jersey house.

"Yeah? What can I do for you?"

"Are you Jack Hudson?"

"Yeah, that's me."

"We're from the Collections Division," said the man with the badge. "We're here to collect your furniture."

"Collect my WHAT?"

"And your cars," said the other. "Please give us the keys."

"This must be a joke," said Hudson, smiling.

"It ain't April Fool's Day," said badge man.

"But, but this is ridiculous—I've never even been audited!"

Hudson's smile was gone.

"We have nothing to do with audits," said big foot. "Another division."

"Look, if I owe money to the IRS, tell me how much. I'll call my accountant . . ."

"It's too late for that," said badge man. "And nothing to do with us. We have a job to do."

"Daddy? What's going on?" Hudson's 12 year-old daughter peeked from behind.

Hudson turned around. "Nothing, honey. It'll be okay." He turned back to the two men at the door, but badge man was already pushing past him, into the house.

"Hey, wait a minute!" Hudson grabbed badge man's arm.

Big foot swung into action, gripping Hudson's neck from behind in a head-lock.

"Daddy! Daddy!" screamed the little girl. "What are they doing!?"

"Officer!" badge man called to the cop, still out-side. "Arrest this man for assault and battery!"

Hudson's wife Susie appeared. "Jack? What's going on?"

"These men say they're from the IRS," hollered Hudson. "They say they're here to take our furni-ture!"

"Why?"

"I haven't the slightest idea!"

"Officer, why are you arresting my husband?"

"Assault on a federal officer is a serious offense, ma'am. You'd best let these men get on with their job." The policeman began reading Hudson his rights.

"Wait a second, darn it! All I did was put my hand on his arm. He's trespassing!"

"Please come quietly, Mr. Hudson. He has every right to enter your house."

"What? I'm not leaving these men in my house with my family!"

The policeman unhooked his radio phone from his belt and spoke into it. A second policeman climbed out of the cruiser and trotted up the path. The officers handcuffed Hudson, sandwiched him between them-selves and swept him out across the threshold. Hudson let his legs collapse. The officers, undeterred, dragged their prisoner out.

"You can't do this!" Hudson yelled. "Susie, phone Bernie Hewitt. Tell them what's happening!"

Hudson had a sense that his neighbors—at least

a half-dozen of them—were watching this spectacle through their windows.

The officers pushed Hudson's head down to squeeze him through the door, into the backseat. They slammed the door and locked it. One officer climbed in behind the wheel. The other returned to the house. Hudson strained his neck for a last look as the cruiser backed out of the driveway. He saw his daughter, a horrified look on her face—and it became a freeze-frame memory etched onto his brain, as if with a hot soldering iron.

Jack Hudson assumed it was morning, though he had no way of knowing in a cell two floors below ground level. His watch had been confiscated when he was booked, photographed and finger-printed the night before—along with his wedding ring, keys and shoelaces, lest he try to hang himself.

Hudson heard rustling outside. A slot in the door bolted open and a bowl of oatmeal appeared.

"Breakfast," grunted a prison guard.

Hudson had hardly slept, racking his brain throughout the long night for something, anything, that would make sense of his predicament. He could think of nothing, his mind always returning to the look on his daughter's face.

Hours and hours later—so it seemed—a guard rustled outside. Was it lunchtime? The cell door opened.

"Come with me," the guard ordered.

Hudson walked numbly down a long corridor. The guard trailed behind, truncheon at the ready. Hudson stood by as the guard cautiously unlocked a door, opened it, and gestured him through.

"Bernie!" Hudson's voice trembled. "How is my wife?"

"She's gone to a hotel with the kids."

"A hotel? Which hotel? Why?"

"They're okay, Jack. They're at the Molly Pitcher Inn. Susie's making arrangements for her parents in Pennsylvania to come pick them up."

"Why?"

"The IRS emptied your house of furniture. And they took your van and car."

"Why? Why?"

"That's what I want to find out from you."

"There's nothing to find out from me! Two men come to my house with the police and barge in. Next thing I know, they're putting me in handcuffs!"

"Okay, okay. Let's go back a bit. You file a tax return, right?"

"Every April."

"When were you audited?"

"I've *never* been audited!"

"Not audited? Are you sure?"

"Of course I'm sure! Phone my accountant if you don't believe me!"

"I believe you. What's your accountant's name?"

"Doug Willoughby."

"Jack, the IRS claims that you owe $75,542 in back taxes . . ."

"What? No way!"

"They made a jeopardy assessment against you."

"A what?"

"If the IRS believes you might try to hide your assets or leave the country, they can make a jeopardy assessment and take everything. It gets turned over to the Collections Division. And it's within their rights to confiscate your property in lieu of unpaid taxes . . ."

"If I owe any money—which I doubt—I sure don't know about it. Aren't they supposed to ask for the money before they charge in like storm troopers?"

"Yes. That's why this is so strange. The Collections Division gets its orders only after many requests are made to you to settle your account. But once Collections gets the order, there's no turning back."

"But they never made any request for money!"

"Okay. I'm going to phone your accountant, confirm what you're saying in writing from him, then I'll find a good tax lawyer to represent you."

"A tax lawyer? Why can't *you* represent me?"

"Look, you need a tax lawyer, a specialist. They know how to deal with the IRS. Trust me, I know what I'm talking about."

"But how much is a tax lawyer?"

"The good ones start at about $250 per hour."

Hudson covered his face with the palms of his

hands. "Oh, Jesus. I thought a man was innocent in this country until proven guilty?"

"Not when the IRS is involved. Now, this other matter . . ."

"What other matter?"

"You're going to be arraigned today for assault and battery. Did you strike someone last night?"

"Hell, no! One of those goons pushed past me, into my house. I just put my hand up to stop him. It was nothing. And then the police put me in handcuffs in front of my children—I can't believe this is happening!"

"Did your hand make contact with the IRS agent?"

"I guess so. My hand brushed against him, that's all."

Bernie shook his head. "That's all they need. Assault against a federal officer in the commission of his duty can get you a jail sentence."

"Oh, Jesus. What do we do?"

"I can help you on that matter. I'll be at the arraignment. Plead not guilty. We'll get you out on bail."

"When?"

"Later today, I hope. You don't have any kind of criminal record, do you?"

"Of course not, Bernie! We've known each other for ten years!"

"I know, I know—but you never know what can turn up. It's better that I know in advance."

"There's nothing to know. Period."

"Good. That's what I wanted to hear."

Jack Hudson was escorted by two federal marshals into the Monmouth County courthouse. He wore handcuffs. Bernie Hewitt sidled up to Hudson who glanced up at the austere judge.

"I have some good news," whispered Bernie.

Hudson exhaled deeply. Relief.

The judge consulted with the prosecution attorney. Bernie was summoned and he stepped forward. Seconds later, he stepped back.

"You are charged with assaulting a federal agent," the judge addressed Hudson. "How do you plead?"

"Not guilty, your honor."

Judge Royce Bambers noted this.

"Your honor, I would like to request bail for my client."

Judge Bambers peered down at the prosecutor.

"We have no objection," said the prosecutor.

Judge Bambers set bond at $5,000.

Bernie requested a lower amount.

"Assaulting a federal officer is a grave offense in my court. Five thousand dollars. I will see you in my courtroom"—the judge checked his calendar and made a notation—"in six weeks—September 16th."

Hudson turned to his attorney. "Do I get to leave now?"

"Soon. A few procedural matters. I'll send a bondsman over to post bail."

"What is the good news you mentioned?"

"The IRS made a mistake."

"Of course they made a mistake! That's what I was trying to tell them!"

The marshals guided Jackson toward the exit.

"I'll be back to pick you up," said Bernie.

Two hours later, a guard appeared outside Hudson's cell.

"Come with me," the guard commanded.

"Thank God. Is my lawyer here?"

"No." The guard was curt. "Telephone."

Hudson was led to a small room. The guard stood by as Hudson raised the phone to his face.

"I have the director of the FBI for you," said a female voice.

"What?"

The next voice Hudson heard belonged to Bryant Westgate.

"What are you doing here?" asked Westgate.

"Excuse me?"

"You heard. What are you *doing* here?"

"In jail?" Hudson was puzzled.

"No. In this book."

"I don't understand . . ."

"You're in the wrong book!" hollered Westgate. "Get out immediately!"

"What do you mean, the *wrong book*?

"Exactly what I said. You have no place here. You're a mistake. Get out. Now!"

"Hold on just a second," snapped Hudson. "First I'm wrongly accused by the IRS and locked up by the cops. And now the FBI wants to take away my existence? This is ridiculous. Are you really the director?"

"Yes," said Westgate. "And you're right, this is ridiculous. So don't keep this going a minute longer—just get out!"

"Or what?"

"I'll tell you what: I report this to the writer—and he'll erase you."

"How?"

"I don't know. Any way he wants. Painfully if you don't hurry."

Hudson said nothing.

"Are you going?" demanded Westgate.

"No. I want to go home to my wife and kids. And I want all my furniture back."

"I don't have the power to do that."

"Then forget it. I'm staying."

"Hold on. I'm going to phone the writer for a conference call." Westgate dialed my number.

"Hello?" This was me.

"Hey you, behind the keyboard—we've got a situation here. A guy named Jack Hudson has turned up in this book. There's no place for him. I told him this, but he refuses to leave."

"Are you sure?" I asked.

"Of course I'm sure. I'm your FBI director."

"Hudson?" I said.

"Yes?" It was a meek, apprehensive yes.

"Shit, it is you! How did you get in here? Never mind. I think Director Westgate is right. You're supposed to be in my *next* book. Would you mind stepping out and I'll try to get back to you next year?"

"No." Hudson was defiant, mustering what little strength he still possessed after his grueling experience. "You have me arrested in front of my family, put me in jail, and now you say I don't even have a right to be here? No. I'm here. And I'm staying. I can't take responsibility for the impulsiveness of your subconscious."

"Look," I said, losing patience. "If you don't bow out gracefully, my next book will be about someone else entirely."

"I'm staying."

"But I can *write* you out."

"Exactly!" confirmed Westgate. "He can *write* you out."

"I'll take my chances." Hudson put down the phone.

"He hung up on us," said Westgate.

"Okay," I said. "Supposing two of your agents murder him?"

"Are you crazy? Don't implicate my Bureau in

murdering anybody! We have enough trouble without getting blamed for that!"

"Look," I said. "He hung up, he's gone. Let's
just forget about him—maybe he'll disappear on his
own. Anyway, we have the opportunity to be creative
here."

"I don't follow " said Westgate.

"What if . . ." I was thinking aloud. "What if I
send Hudson back in time, have him drive down to
Washington and crash into that Kurd on 10th Street
before he massacres your agents?"

"You can do that?"

"I can do anything I want. I'm the writer,
remember?"

"Do it!"

I thought about it for several seconds. "Nah," I
said. "This book isn't about time travel."

"You're teasing me."

"You're the FBI director. Solve your own goddam
problems." I put down the phone, intrigued by what
had just transpired.

3

Tom Washburn looked out of the picture window of his fourth floor office onto Grosvenor Square. A pigeon sat upon Franklin Roosevelt's head. It had been a rainy summer in London. But, despite the need for a raincoat and umbrella most days, Washburn lamented that his two-year stint as CIA chief of station was almost at an end. London was his swan song—a reward for 30 years of service in far less desirable foreign capitals, and at headquarters in Langley. Ahead of him, semi-retirement, a little consulting, maybe some contract work from his old employer. All things considered, Washburn preferred London to Washington. The theatre, the museums, and the lush parks had transformed him into an Anglophile, cultivating a taste for tweed jackets and afternoon tea at Fortnum & Mason.

But today, as was his custom on Friday, Washburn wished to satisfy a craving for American food.

Washburn pressed his intercom button.

"Jenny? Hard Rock Cafe?"

"Fine."

It was only 11:30, but Washburn had learned from experience—get to the Hard Rock before noon if you didn't want to stand in a queue. An early lunch suited him fine—Washburn had been in the office since 7:30.

Jenny Hills had been in London 18 months longer than Washburn, having first served his predecessor as secretary and personal assistant. With Washburn, her role had broadened to mistress—another reason Washburn liked London and didn't wish to leave. Maybe he would go into some kind of business? An antiquarian book service perhaps? This thought crossed Washburn's mind as he adjusted his trenchcoat.

Jenny was ready when Washburn exited his office. The pair quietly left the high-security wing of the fourth floor, a clacking of titter-tatter behind them. Their stealthy liaison was no secret in a department where secrets were tightly kept. It seemed everyone had a need to know that Washburn was poking his secretary. And that he did so early Friday afternoons at the nearby Britannia Hotel.

Tom and Jenny removed their security badges, negotiated the steps outside the large embassy and turned right onto South Audley Street, past The Spy Shop and, a few doors further, The Counter Spy Shop. Washburn glanced at a bulletproof vest in one window. That was hardly something he'd need in this most civilized posting.

A right turn on Curzon Street, left on Park Lane, past the London Hilton toward Hyde Park Corner.

As he passed the Hard Rock Cafe's retail shop, Tom Washburn would not have noticed that its window-shoppers included a Kurd named Ahmed Matsalah.

The Hard Rock Cafe occupied a handsome building, originally a Rolls-Royce showroom, on the corner of Old Park Lane and Piccadilly. Tom and Jenny entered the burger emporium and were shown to an upper-level booth in back.

Washburn always sat back to the wall, so he could be in command of his surroundings. A waitress quickly appeared. The Hard Rock made its vast profits by rapid table-turning.

Washburn knew what he wanted: a cheeseburger, medium-rare, Italian dressing on the salad, chocolate shake. For Jenny, a BLT and a vanilla shake.

Ahmed Matsalah pushed his way into the Hard Rock, around a line that had begun to form.

"Excuse me," said a host, blocking Matsalah's path.

"The bar," spat Matsalah.

"Oh. Okay, then." The host pointed. "Up there."

Matsalah turned left and stepped up to the bar.

"What can I get you?" asked the barkeep, an effervescent American.

"Coca-Cola."

Matsalah didn't touch the glass of soda set before him, but surveyed the restaurant and those in it. He focused on Tom Washburn for a long moment, then quickly averted his gaze.

The swarthy young man reached into his coat pocket, which had been altered to accommodate a Skorpion VZ 61. Wordlessly, he left the bar, leaving his Coke undrunk and unpaid for. The barkeep assumed he was headed for the toilet, but kept a watchful eye upon him nonetheless. He watched, distractedly, as Matsalah turned right instead of left, then up a few stairs to the rear booth section.

Tom Washburn never had a chance, never knew what had so abruptly, and dramatically, ended his life. In a quick, passing movement, Matsalah had put his Skorpion to Washburn's temple and fired manually. The CIA station chief's head exploded, despatching soft grey matter and hard bone fragments onto collector guitars bolted to the wall, and onto other diners.

Jenny Hills had hardly a chance to react before Matsalah turned the gun on her, switching to automatic and filling her chest with lead. She slumped over the table, vacant of life.

The American bartender, who had seen it all, hollered to stop the horror. But no one reacted. Except

Matsalah. He turned to the bar and let his Skorpion rip, cutting through bar patrons and liquor bottles and a large mirror behind the bar. Matsalah jumped from the rear booth section and dashed to the bar. The bartender cowered behind it, dripping blood from an arm wound. Matsalah leveled his weapon at the barkeep's head and fired. Another brain and skull explosion.

Matsalah exchanged clips, empty for full, and swung his weapon toward diners on the main floor. Most of them had scrambled to the floor, crawling under tables for cover. The swarthy young man fired indiscriminately at everything that moved—and everyone that didn't move. He kept firing as he made his way to the door. There was no longer a queue outside. Would-be diners had scattered, leaving the pavement eerily deserted. A Volkswagon Golf GTI revved its engine curbside. Matsalah sprinted to the vehicle and jumped in. The small car's tires squealed as it tore around the corner, onto Old Park Lane.

Bryant Westgate had barely removed his coat when he received an urgent call from his legat at the London embassy. Westgate sat frozen as he listened, blood draining from his face. The CIA station chief and his secretary assassinated. At least a dozen others dead. The lone gunman sounded awfully like Ahmed Matsalah. A Skorpion VZ 61 had been left on the scene.

Westgate's phone had barely rested in its cradle for five seconds when it rang again. This time, Carlton Price, Director of Central Intelligence.

"I just lost one of the best men this agency has ever known," Price fumed, "and I want to know what the hell you're going to do about it!"

The two officials had long ago given up the pretense of pleasantries. Ordinarily, they could avoid each other by delegating interagency relations to deputies. But now their lives, their jobs, had sensationally overlapped.

"We had a ransom demand . . ." offered Bryant.

"I know! And not because *you* told me!"

Indignance gripped Bryant at the suggestion that one of his lieutenants would leak anything to the Agency, but there was little point berating Price over this. Westgate was about to respond when his personal fax rang.

"Hold on," said the FBI director. He watched as the fax inched from his machine:

Communique # 2

Our money did not arrive. So we have served a second course.

We are still doing appetizers. You cannot imagine what we are cooking for a main course.

Send 500 Million US today.

Skorpion

"What is it?" Price demanded. "Are you there?"

"Yes. Another ransom demand. It just arrived."

"By fax?"

"Yes."

"Do you know where it's coming from?"

"No."

"Don't you even have Caller ID over there? I'm calling the president."

Price was gone.

"Asshole," muttered Westgate. He slammed the phone and reached for his intercom. "Cheryl, is Jim in yet?"

"I'll check."

"Get him in here as quickly as possible."

Five minutes later Westgate's intercom buzzed. "Is it Jim?"

"No," said Cheryl. "The president."

"Shit. Put him through."

Westgate listened. And listened. And listened.

"Yes, sir," he squeezed in. "Yes, Mr. President. Uh-huh. Yes. Good-bye, Mr. President." Westgate replaced the phone as Jim Thompson knocked and entered.

"Sonofabitch!" said Thompson.

"Tell me about it. I just had the president eating my eardrum."

"Price?"

"Yeah. Every opportunity. The essence was, catch this guy before he kills anyone else—with CIA cooperation."

"An oxymoron?"

"Take it easy, Jim. We're overlapping now whether we like it or not. I don't. But with a mad Kurd on the loose overseas, we've got problems." Westgate wiped his bow. "Your friend, Dalkin. Tell me more about him."

"Best undercover man the Bureau ever had. He's done mob stings, money-laundering—even brothels. He's had so many identities, he doesn't even know who he is anymore. Married once, kids. A road warrior. He travelled so much, when they left him, he didn't find out for six months. He lives for his next assignment. He's a clean slate, a John Doe, until somebody gives him a job with a new identity and a motivation. He's private now. Big jobs for billionaires or multinationals. He doesn't like government. But I can get him."

"What's his downside?"

"He's not a team player. His creativity is not usually appreciated by bureaucracy. And he has Tourette's syndrome."

"So you said. Does it effect his work?"

"It's an advantage."

"How's that?"

"It makes him less suspicious. Eccentricities, physical or mental, are excellent for undercover work. They cause distractions and advance character credibility."

"Can you guarantee that he won't embarrass the Bureau?"

"I can't promise anything except that he's what we need right now—especially since we have the President's support. Tracking this Kurd and apprehending him outside the country is going to get political. With the White House on our side, we've got some flexibility. With your permission, I'll call Dalkin, see if he's around."

"Do it."

Thompson picked up a phone, touch-keyed. It rang twice.

"Ye-ees?" said a voice, on loudspeaker.

"Dalkin?"

"Maybe."

"Jim Thompson."

"Jim-my! You still working for the Federal Bureau of Incompetents?"

"Yes, Dalkin. I have the director with me."

"Oh."

"Can you come see me, Dalkin?"

"When?"

"Tomorrow."

"Okay. What time?"

"Whenever you get here."

"Okay. Bye."

Dalkin was gone. Thompson put the phone back in its cradle.

"*That* was Dalkin?" Westgate raised his eyebrows.

"Yes."

"But he sounds so, so tame, so mousy."

"That's right," said Thompson. "He's probably not working this week."

"What do you mean?"

"I told you. He's bland, vacant—like an empty shell until he assumes a new name, a new identity. He creates a personality to suit the assignment."

Westgate shook his head, unbelieving. His curiosity about Dalkin was pierced by the intercom.

"Carlton Price," said Jenny.

"Shit," said Westgate. "Twice in one day."

Westgate hit the button and listened. His face reddened. "I don't think . . ." He listened, bristled. "If that's the way he wants it."

Westgate replaced the receiver and looked at Thompson, who was waiting expectantly.

"CIA is sending a team to London in pursuit of the Kurd," said Westgate.

"But the Bureau has jurisdiction . . ." said Thompson.

"The President has authorized CIA to run its own investigation, independent of us. 'A contest.' That's what Price called it."

4

"The IRS has apologized." Bernie Hewitt turned his ignition key and drove out of the police carpark.

Jack Hudson stared straight ahead. "Is that all? An apology? Can't we sue for false imprisonment or something?"

"No. Your arrest and imprisonment was for assaulting a federal officer."

"But it was a direct result of their admitted mistake!" Hudson was incredulous. "I was just protecting my property!"

"The law deals with one offense at a time," said Hewitt. "But don't worry. When I describe to the judge what happened, he'll show leniency and only slap your hand. You have a clean record. And we'll show that the IRS blundered—and then maybe we'll sue the government for damages."

"How did it happen?"

"The IRS screwed up on your social security

41

number. Your number ends with 6-9. The guy they were looking for has the same number as you except it ends with 9-6. A computer error."

"I don't fucking believe it!" Hudson shook his head. It was not like him to swear, but these were special circumstances. "I have a question for you, Bernie."

"Shoot."

"Is the Director of the FBI someone named Bryant Westgate?"

"Yeah, I think so. Why?"

"He phoned me."

"Phoned *you*? Why?"

"I *think* he phoned me. Jeez, I don't know, the past 18 hours have been like a nightmare. Maybe I *dreamt* it. But this guy, Westgate, said he's Director of the FBI, and he said I'm in the *wrong book*."

"He said *what*?"

"I'm not making this up. He said, 'You're in the wrong book, please get out,' or something like that."

"The *wrong book*?"

"That's what he said."

"It must have been a hallucination. Did the cops give you a drug of some kind to help you sleep?"

"No. Nothing. It was very real. This guy West-gate, whoever he is, asked me to leave. And get this, then he called someone he said was the *writer...*"

"The *writer*?"

"Right. And this guy the writer said I should leave, too!"

"Absurd."

"That's what I think," said Hudson. "But I didn't know the name of the FBI director till he called—and you've confirmed it."

The lawyer's Motorola car phone rang.

"Hello?" said Bernie.

"This is Bryant Westgate, director of the FBI," announced a voice.

"That's him!" yelled Hudson. "That's the guy who called me!"

"Of course it's me!" said Westgate. "What the hell are you still doing here, Hudson?"

"Hold on a minute," said Hewitt. "I'm Jack Hudson's lawyer—I'll handle this!"

"There's nothing to handle, Hewitt. It's very simple. You're *both* in the wrong book. Get out!"

"We're not going anywhere," said Hewitt. "I'm driving Mr. Hudson home."

"Exactly! And that's the end of your story. You no longer have a place in this book. You never did, but the writer says it's too late to do anything about that now."

"On the contrary, Mr. Westgate, if you *are* the real director of the FBI—and believe me, I'm going to check—we're not finished yet."

"What do you mean, 'not finished yet'?"

"My client has a number of options to keep his story spinning."

"No," said Westgate. "Hudson's a bore and you know it. This is the only exciting thing that's happened to him his whole life—and now it's over."

"I resent that!" hollered Hudson.

"Shhh," Bernie admonished. "Let me handle this." He returned his attention to Westgate. "I don't know who you think you are . . ."

"I'm the director of the FBI. I've already consulted the writer on this, and he agrees. Hudson has to leave this book immediately."

"We're not going anywhere," said Hewitt. "Take us to court." He hit a button and disconnected Westgate.

"See! I wasn't dreaming!" said Hudson. "What the hell is going on here?"

"It sounds hokey to me," said Hewitt. "It may be a stupid prank, one of your neighbors, a friend, an enemy who heard about your situation. Don't worry, I'll call the local FBI office when I get to my office and report this. It's against the law to impersonate a federal officer."

The phone rang again. Hewitt answered.

"This is the director of the FBI . . ."

"Stick it in your ear, buster!" Hewitt disconnected Westgate as he pulled into the Molly Pitcher Inn forecourt. "Susie is in room 217."

"When do we get to go home?"

"The IRS said it'll be a week or two before they can get your furniture back . . ."

"*A week or two?* Why so long?"

"It's a bureaucratic thing. They said they'll schedule it as soon as possible, but they're booked up. I'm supposed to call this afternoon for a confirmed date."

"This is ridiculous! Are they paying my hotel bill?"

"I doubt it. But I'll see if I can get *something* out of them for the inconvenience caused you."

Hudson shook his head. "I don't believe this! What about my van and my car?"

"They said they'll return them with your furniture."

"You mean I have to rent a car now?"

"I'll ask them to find you a loaner, but don't hold your breath. The IRS likes to *receive* money, not dish it out."

Hudson alighted from the car, dazed, in shock, and entered the lobby. All be wanted was to see his wife and hug his daughters.

"He's still here." Bryant Westgate was speaking to me on the phone.

"Who?"

"You know damn well who!"

"Don't swear at *me*, Bryant."

"I'm the director of the FBI!" hollered Westgate. "You're just some friggin' writer who can't get his stories straight . . ."

Bryant Westgate started to pee in his pants. Urine soaked through flannel trousers and dripped down his legs . . .

"No! No!" Bryant shrieked. "Don't . . ."

The pee-pee stopped.

"Holy Christ!" yelled Westgate. "Look what you've done!" He looked down at dark, soppy patch on his crotch.

"Don't give me that *friggin' writer* stuff," I said. "Things are tough enough for writers without getting told off by their own characters, for chrissakes. But *you*, sir—you'd better have some respect. I can have the President phone you in thirty seconds and fire your ass. Between you and me, he's already thinking about it."

"Really? How do you know?"

"Because he thinks what I want him to think. And because Carlton Price is trying to get you replaced."

"That bastard! Hmmm, I bet if you wanted, you could do something about Price, uh, maybe get *him* replaced?"

"Sure I could," I said. "But I'm not going to do that. It's not part of my story. Solve your own problems—including Hudson."

"But Hudson's *your* problem! He's muddying *your* book!"

"I can live with that. You're the one who's having a cow about it."

"What about the readers?"

"What readers?"

"The people who read this book."

"What about them?"

"They're going to be confused, even irritated."

"If I was writing for readers, I wouldn't write. Nobody reads books anymore. And if they read this one, and they're confused or irritated or both, tough donkey dicks. I'm writing this for myself, because I can't not write."

"So, you're saying I'm wasting my time as FBI director?"

"I didn't say that," I said. "But if you don't want the job, resign and I'll give it to somebody else."

"Wait a minute, has the CIA set this up?"

"Set what up?"

"You. You're talking me out of my job."

"Paranoid, aren't we."

"Look, I want to be FBI director. I want to be in this book. I just can't understand why this guy Hudson keeps popping up and you don't do anything about it."

"Have you ever thought that maybe there's a reason Hudson is here? I mean, you really do have a helluva lot of nerve, one, to order him out and, two, to tell me to erase him. Who ever heard of a character calling the writer to tell him who to include and who not to include? If this keeps up, I'm going to write you out completely, Bryant. I'll shelve this story about you and that Kurd, and make this a book about Hudson and the IRS. I can do that. You can't arrest me. You can't prosecute me. Nothing. Do you understand who's in charge here?"

"I guess." Westgate was sheepish.

The director of the FBI backed off. It gave me pause. Here I was, a lowly writer, telling America's top cop where to get off. And he *had* to listen. And it dawned on me: When I'm sitting in front of a keyboard, I'm in charge. I can do anything I want, make anything happen. I can bring Santo Trafficante back from the dead.

"Santo, I command your spirit to appear!"

Moments later, the ghost of Santo Trafficante stood before me.

"Santo, you Italian prick, tell me the truth about JFK."

"I can no say."

"You're dead, a ghost, and now I've captured your soul on this page, and you'll answer my questions or I'll have your body exhumed and deliver it to a pig farm."

"Si. I tell you about Gianni."

"You do that."

"We should have hit Bobby, not Gianni. Carlo say . . ."

"Carlo?"

"Carlo Marcello. He say, we cut off the head of the serpent. But Carlo wrong. It was mistake to hit Gianni."

"Who fired the shots?" I asked.

Trafficante said nothing.

"The triggermen," I said. "Who were they?"

"One named Roberto, I dunno last name. The other, Sergio. Sergio Arcacha Smith. Cubans. They supposed to work for me. Me and Carlo."

"And Oswald."

"I dunno Oswald. I not bother with details. The SOBs double-crossed me and Carlo."

"Oswald?"

"No, Oswald. Roberto and Sergio."

"What do you mean?"

"Sergio live in Havana now. He first person to cross from Texas to Mexico when they reopen the border 48 hours after the hit. Then he flies to Cuba—the only passenger on a Cubanair flight."

"What are you saying?"

"You figure it out."

"Castro?"

"I kill that greasy, lying bastard with my bare hands. We're waiting for him down here."

"Okay, hold on—let's take a back-step. Why didn't the FBI go after you?"

"Eddie happy to see Gianni gone . . ."

"Eddie?"

"Eddie Hoover. Eddie never worry about the families. Eddie know we keep our business in the family and look after our own, keep order our way. Eddie used to trade tips with Frankie . . ."

"Frankie?"

"Frankie Costello. They good friends. They bet horses. Also, we know about Junior."

"Who?"

"Clyde. Clyde Tolson. Eddie call him 'Junior.' Eddie and Junior—a pair of faggots. We have pictures. Eddie and Junior not bother Carlo and me. And, anyway, Eddie more interested in keeping the niggers in their place . . ."

"Don't use the word 'nigger,' Santo."

"You bring me here and ask questions, I tell you. That's how I talk. You no like, bite me. Eddie also calls them niggers . . ."

My phone rang. It was Bryant Westgate.

"You again?" I was starting to get annoyed.

"I object!" Westgate objected. "J. Edgar Hoover was the founding director of the FBI. Our *headquarters* is named after him. You're giving this hood a platform to defile Mr. Hoover's memory."

"You calling me a hood?" said Trafficante.

"You just admitted you're the guy who assassinated Kennedy!" hollered Westgate. "'Hood' is being kind!"

"And you think Eddie the Faggot deserves to have a building named after him?" said Trafficante. "After what he do to Hale Boggs? I got some stories . . ."

"I don't want to hear them!" yelled Westgate. "I just want to get on with this book!"

"Okay, Santo," I said. "Piss off."

Santo Trafficante was gone.

"Happy now?" I asked Westgate.

"I'd be happier you would edit out your dialogue with that, that mafioso."

"Why? In one page of fiction I've dredged up more about who killed Kennedy than 2,000 blowhard nonfiction books. It's true what Trafficante said, isn't it?"

Westgate said nothing.

"I want an answer, Bryant."

"Yes, it's true."

The director of the FBI confirmed Santo Trafficante's posthumous admission.

"And Bobby, too?"

"Don't drag me into this."

5

Bernie Hewitt picked up the phone in his office and touch-keyed a number.

"FBI," said a voice.

"Is Dick Preston there?" asked Bernie.

"Hold on. I'll transfer you."

"Dick Preston speaking."

"Dick," said Bernie. "Bernie Hewitt. Could you check something out for me?"

"Hi, Bernie. What it is?"

"Somebody's been calling a client of mine saying that he's Bryant Westgate."

"Our director?"

"That's right. He called twice. Probably a crank. He says my client is in the wrong book and, by extension, me, too."

"The wrong book?"

"I know. Weird, isn't it?"

"What's your client's name?"

"Hudson. Jack Hudson."

Preston scribbled the name on a legal pad. "Hang tight. I'll check with headquarters on this and call you back."

Bryant Westgate was sitting at his desk, inspecting a glob of green mucous he'd just picked from his nose. His intercom buzzed.

"What is it Cheryl?"

"I've got Jim Thompson and Jeff Dalkin here."

"Hold on, hold on." Westgate grabbed a Kleenex tissue and wiped his finger clean. "Okay. Send them in."

Thompson entered the office. Jeff Dalkin was a step behind. Westgate did a double take.

"Jeff Dalkin." Thompson introduced Dalkin to the director.

Westgate shook hands with Dalkin. "You look *exactly* like Bruce Willis," said Westgate. "Did anybody ever tell you that?"

Dalkin shook his head, a goofy smile gracing his cocky countenance. "Yeah, I get told that a lot. Crinkum-crankum, pop-a-nut."

"It's uncanny," said Westgate. "You could be his double."

"Yeah, I know. Blow me. I get calls from celebrity look-alike agencies. They wanna pay me 500 bucks a day to turn up at parties. Dirty bottoms."

"Sit down, sit down," said Westgate, seating himself behind his large desk and facing the two men.

"I've briefed Dalkin on the situation," said Thompson. "He says he's willing to take the assignment."

"Good, good," said Westgate, still absorbed by Dalkin's likeness to the famous movie star.

"Sturimo Stoots," said Dalkin. "Cocksucking Kurds. Scum."

"Wha . . .?" Westgate bit his tongue, remembering Dalkin's disability. Westgate handed copies of the two faxes across his desk to Dalkin. "Look at these."

Dalkin read. "Hmmm. Extortion. Have the Swiss been of any help? Whoremongering mutherfucks."

"We have our legat in Berne working on it," said Westgate. "We're getting the usual Swiss run-around."

"Even in this case? Pimp-puke."

"That's the Swiss. They'd rather bank our 500 million than reveal an extortionist. No, that's unfair. But they have quote-unquote 'procedures' to protect their reputation for numbered accounts."

"Numbered accounts, numbered accounts," echoed Dalkin. "Whoremongering cunt-faced fart-licking Swiss cheese—cut the fucking cheese—no-farting-please sons-of-bitches."

Westgate froze. Dalkin smiled sheepishly. Tourette's.

Jeff Dalkin boarded Swissair's only flight out of Dulles, to Zurich, and took his seat in Business Class.

A stewardess rushed over. "Mr. Willis? Is there anything I can get you?"

"Uh, no, I'm not Bruce Willis. Crinkum-crankum, pop-a-nut."

"Really? You look exactly like him."

"I know. I hear that a lot. Dirty bottoms."

The large jumbo was virtually empty until it reached Boston, where it filled with passengers and took off for the long haul across the Atlantic. During the short night, Jeff Dalkin sipped red wine and grew into a new frame of mind. He would still be Jeff Dalkin—that's what his passport said, and the letter from Bryant Westgate confirming that he was acting on behalf of the U.S. Government at its highest level. He took his motivation from the letter. Tough guy, yeah.

By the time the jet touched down, Dalkin was walking with a swagger. He swaggered through Immigration and Customs and hopped into a taxi.

"The Savoy, Paridisplatz," he said. His voice now had an edge to it; an edge that said, the most direct route, punk.

Dalkin swaggered into the Savoy, checked in, hung his garment bag in the closet and consulted the telephone directory. Headquarters for the Union Bank of Switzerland was within yodeling distance, on nearby Bahnhofstrasse. Dalkin jotted the address on Savoy notepaper. His phone buzzed. Dalkin checked his watch. Eleven a.m. Dalkin picked up the receiver.

"Yeah?"

"Steve Duffy. I'm the . . ."

"Yeah, yeah, Steve—I know who you are. C'mon up. Room 412."

Duffy was attached to the Legat's office in Berne.

A knock at the door. Dalkin opened. "C'mon in, siddown." He motioned to the chair, punching at it.

Duffy stared at Dalkin. "Jeez, you look just like Bruce Willis."

"Crinkum crankum, pop-a-nut," said Dalkin. "Bruce shit, piss and puke Willis!"

"Sorry," said Duffy.

"Sorry, sorry, sorry," said Dalkin. "Please sit, Sturimo Stoots."

"No, I'm Steve Duffy." Duffy sat stiffly in an upholstered armchair, his eyes fixed upon Dalkin.

"Bring me up to speed, Steve." Dalkin leaned against a desk, arms crossed.

"We've made an application through the Swiss Government to get UBS to reveal the name of the account holder," said Duffy.

"When was that?"

"One week ago."

"And?"

"It takes time."

"How much time?"

"Three weeks, a month."

"By which time the account holder gets tipped off, closes the account, opens another."

"They've assured me . . ."

"Yeah, yeah. Assurances. Jerk the turkey, milk the chicken. Look, I don't have time, Steve. I want a meeting today with the highest ranking official at UBS."

"I don't know if the Swiss Government . . ."

"I don't give a broccoli fart about the Swiss government, whoremongering pecksniffs—this is between me and the bank. Call now." Dalkin lifted the phone from the desk and passed it to Duffy. "Here's the number." He handed the notepad to Duffy.

Duffy was hesitant. "If I say I'm from the embassy and I want a meeting for a visiting official from the Bureau, they're going to say, 'Call the government.'"

"So don't say that."

"What do you *want* me to say?"

"Say you've got an extremely wealthy American businessman in town who wants to open an account."

"But it's not true."

"No," said Dalkin. "So what?"

"It, it'll rebound on me!"

"No. I'll take full responsibility. Go ahead and call."

"But, but, they'll think it's odd that a representative of the U.S. government is assisting with the opening of a account, won't they?"

"Not at all. They'll assume it's the CIA—cuntfarts—laundering money for an operation."

"Oh." The assistant legat gulped and reluctantly touch-keyed the number. He spoke German to an operator, then cupped his hand over the mouthpiece. "She's connecting me with the General Manager."

"General Manager, General Manager," echoed Dalkin. "Willie Wanker whacking his wong." He jerked his head back, then snapped it up straight. "Stoots McGoots!"

Duffy shook his head, wondering what he'd gotten himself into. He removed his hand from the phone and spoke more German. He listened, then scribbled something onto the notepad. He put the receiver down.

"You have an appointment at two p.m.," said Duffy.

"You mean *we*. You're coming, too."

"Me?" Duffy choked. "Why me?"

"I may need you to translate. Can you recommend some place to eat? I'm famished."

"Uh, down the street. A place called Kropf."

"Kropf, Kropf, Kropf," echoed Dalkin. "Let's go to Kropf."

Dalkin ordered the lunch special, speck and sauerkraut, and it immediately became part of his Tourettic repertoire.

"Speck and sauerkraut," said Dalkin. "Speck and sauerkraut."

"Why do you keep saying that?" asked Duffy.

"Saying what?"

"Speck and sauerkraut."

"Do I?" Dalkin pointed his right fist outward and punched the air, once, twice, three times. "Wanking wieners! Goddam-fucking speck and sauerkraut!"

Duffy excused himself to use the toilet—he said—and found a pay phone. He dropped a coin into the box, dialed the embassy in Berne and asked for extension 216.

"Don? It's me Steve. I'm in Zurich with this guy Dalkin, who's really weird, and he's getting us into a very unconventional situation . . ."

"I don't want to know the details," the legal attache cut in. "Our instructions are to assist Mr. Dalkin with whatever he asks."

"But he's . . ."

"Period."

Duffy put the phone back in its cradle and returned to Dalkin.

"Speck and sauerkraut," said Dalkin. He shoved the last piece of speck into his mouth and washed it down with beer. He checked his watch. One-thirty. "C'mon, let's get there early."

Duffy led Dalkin around the corner to Bahnhofstrasse, Zurich's main avenue, bustling with shoppers, businessmen and trolley cars; its shop windows were resplendent with fine watches and crocodile luggage and homemade chocolates in fancy wrappings.

"Ritzy-titzy," said Dalkin. "Ritzy-titzy-titzy-tits.

Torpedo tits. Boobs. Booooobs! Big bodacious bazonking boobs . . ."

"Zurich is an elegant city." Duffy, conscious of being gaped at by passersby, was purple. "One of every 30 residents is a millionaire."

"I'm not surprised with the prices they charge."

Minutes later, the two men stood outside the Union Bank of Switzerland. Dalkin looked up and down the street, absorbing everything like a sponge— or so it seemed to Duffy.

They entered through the stainless steel and glass revolving door—sparkling and sterile—and approached the receptionist.

"Mr. Frey, please," Duffy said, in German.

"Do you have an appointment?"

"Yes. Steve Duffy and Jeff Dalkin."

"Please sit over there." The receptionist pointed to a leather couchette.

The pair sat. Dalkin inspected several slick investment brochures spread out before him on the glass coffee table. Funds and futures and currencies and metals.

"Mr. Duffy?" the receptionist spoke in English. "Mr. Frey will see you now. Take zee elevator to zee fource floor. Someone will meet you."

"Thank you."

"What are you going to say?" Duffy asked nervously as the elevator ascended. He tried to mask his apprehension with nonchalance.

"I don't know yet. That's why I wanted to get here early—to get a feeling for what makes this place tick."

"Simple," said Duffy. "Money."

"It's deeper," said Dalkin. "It's *people* with money."

"Yeah, I guess." Duffy just wanted to get whatever Dalkin had in mind wrapped up as quickly as possible, get on a train and return to quiet, peaceful Berne.

Bryant Westgate, seated at his large mahogany desk, picked up the phone and dialed my number.

I answered.

"That was a cheap trick," said Westgate.

"What, having you pick your nose?"

"No. And stop doing that! I'm talking about how you described Jeff Dalkin as a Bruce Willis look-alike."

"How's that?" I asked.

"You know very well. You got out of describing a character."

"Bollocks. In my mind's eye Dalkin looks *exactly* like Bruce Willis."

"So you said. I still think it's cheap and unprofessional."

Westgate put down the phone and ran to his private toilet to unleash a violent stream of diarrhea. This popped his cluster of very ripe hemorrhoids and he couldn't sit down the rest of the afternoon.

"Ah, Mr. Duffy, Mr. Dalkin." Reymond Frey, General Manager of UBS, greeted the two Americans. "Please—come into my office."

Frey stood by the door in his dark suit and sober demanor. He gestured the men to sit down, then closed the door and took position behind his immaculate desk, not a paper clip out of place.

"I have prepared the forms for a new account." Frey pushed a sheaf of paper across his desk toward Dalkin. "Under normal circumstances, I would need a photocopy of your passport, but we'll waive that in this instance." Frey winked a knowing wink—the same wink he gave to a Russian opening a KGB account one week earlier. "How much do you wish to deposit?"

"Actually, Mr. Frey," said Dalkin. "I don't want to open an account today. Brain-fart."

"I don't understand," said Frey.

"I'll explain. Blow me. The reason for this meeting is that I want you to tell me the name of the individual who has *this* account with your bank." Dalkin pulled a scrap of notepaper from his shirt pocket and pushed it across the desk.

"I can not do this." Frey spoke with great indignance, refusing to even glance at the scrap of paper before him. "You have intruded on my time, my office, under this, this false pretense."

Duffy, embarrassed, tried to lose himself in his buttery leather chair.

"It would be in your best interest to do what I ask," said Dalkin.

"I cannot." Frey stood up, signaling an end to their meeting.

Dalkin remained seated. "Yes you can. Access this account on your computer, write down the name to whom it belongs and hand it to me. The whole process will take you less than 30 seconds."

"This is a matter for our governments..."

"No," said Dalkin. "This is between you and me. Pop-a-nut."

"Swiss banking secrecy is a very strict matter." Frey spoke sternly. "You must follow the correct procedures..."

"Let me make this real simple, Mr. Frey, because I don't have all day to spar with you about correct procedures. I want you to be very clear on what I'm going to do if you don't give me a name. Dogs vomit. I'm going to put agents outside every branch of UBS throughout Switzerland, throughout Europe, and we're going to take pictures of every customer who walks in and out of your bank. Then I'm going to leak what we're doing to friendly reporters at the *Wall Street Journal* and the *International Herald Tribune*, along with the names and faces of account holders we identify. And I'll make sure your name gets in there, too—in bold print. Pimps and whores."

Frey looked at Steve Duffy. "He can do this?"

Duffy shrugged. "My instructions are, he can do whatever he wants."

"But, but this is blackmail." Frey lowered his rump into his chair.

"Not at all," said Dalkin. "We've been considering this kind of operation to help our friends at DEA and the IRS. You're just giving me a starting point. Crinkum-crankum."

Frey sat stiffly for a few moments. He swiveled in his chair, clacked his computer keyboard, consulted the screen, then swept his Mont Blanc pen across a notepad. Without looking at either of the men, he pushed his scribble toward Dalkin.

"Good day, *gentlemen*." Frey brusquely saw them out the door.

Dalkin pocketed the note and stood up. "Speck and sauerkraut," he said.

"Oh my God," Steven Duffy shook his head and muttered as he and Dalkin walked along Bahnhofstrasse. "That guy was pissed off. He's gonna have our asses. Oh, man, my career is ruined!"

"He's not gonna do shit," said Dalkin.

"What makes you so sure?"

"Simple: He just broke his country's very strict bank secrecy laws by giving me this name."

"Oh." Duffy stopped in his tracks and pondered this. "Yeah, that's right!" He picked up his pace again. "We're okay! Whew!" Duffy dabbed as his sweaty brow with a handkerchief. What's the name he gave you?"

Dalkin pulled the note from his pocket to look at it for the first time. He gasped. "Fuck-fuck-fuck-fuck-fuck-fuck-fuck-fuck!"

Bernie Hewitt's phone rang.

"Bernie? Dick Preston."

"Hi, Dick. Thanks for getting back to me so soon."

"Look, Bernie, this is kind of embarrassing. You know that I'm normally happy to do favors for you . . ."

"And you know I appreciate it."

"I know, I know . . . but I've been instructed not to talk about the issue you asked about."

"Why not?"

"There's some confusion at headquarters. I've been told not to touch it."

"What confusion? I just want to know if your director phoned my client."

Preston hesitated. "Uh, yes, that's correct."

"So we're in the wrong book?"

"That's what I can't talk about."

"Why not?"

"Look, Bernie, I'd like to help you—but I'm supposed to leave this alone."

"Well, what should I *do*?"

"I don't know. Really. I'm sorry."

"Are we breaking any *law* by being in this book?"

"I don't know of any law that applies. It's about as grey an area as ever existed. But, please, I can't get involved, okay?"

"All right. Thanks anyway, Dick."

6

J eff Dalkin huddled with Jim Thompson and Bryant Westgate inside the director's office.

"You're not going to believe who that bank account belongs to," said Dalkin, shaking his head. It was late afternoon and he had just returned to Washington from Switzerland.

"Saddam Hussein?" said Thompson.

"Muammar Ghaddafy?" said Westgate.

"No," said Dalkin. "Henry Kissinger of Kissinger Associates." He slapped Reymond Frey's notepaper onto Westgate's desk. "Speck and sauerkraut."

"I don't believe it," said Westgate. "Are you sure you have the right account?"

They double-checked the account number on both faxes received by Westgate. It was correct.

"That Swiss banker must be playing a joke on you," said Westgate.

"I don't think so," said Dalkin. "Speck and sauerkraut."

"Then the real account holder must be playing a joke on the bank," said Westgate.

"Maybe," said Dalkin. "Kiss ass, kiss ass, goddam-heinie-fart-face! Speck and sauerkraut!"

Westgate ignored Dalkin's outburst and picked up his phone. "Cheryl, get me Henry Kissinger of Kissinger Associates in New York."

"Yes, Mr. Westgate."

Westgate put the phone down and turned to Thompson. "We'll get to the bottom of this."

The phone rang.

"I have Dr. Kissinger," said Cheryl.

"Thank you, Cheryl—put him through."

"Henry? How are you?"

Westgate listened impassively as Kissinger droned in a deep gravelly voice about his annual visit to Bohemian Grove in the American redwoods. "Sounds great, Henry. Yes, I'd love to be your guest out there sometime, thank you. Uh, I have a small matter I need to discuss with you. Could you come down to Washington?" Westgate listened. "Yes, I know how busy you are, Henry, but it really is quite important that we talk as soon as possible." Westgate listened. "A month from Wednesday? No, that really is too far away." Westgate listened. "No, this isn't a consulting arrangement. We can't pay you. No, Henry—that won't do. Henry? Henry?" Westgate put down the phone. "That sonofabitch hung up on me!"

"Arrest him," said Dalkin.

"Arrest Henry Kissinger?"

"Yeah, arrest Henry kiss ass, kiss ass—you know who I mean. We've linked his name to an account that's being used to massacre people and extort 500 million dollars from the US Government."

"I *did* give him the opportunity to come down and talk about this," said Westgate. "Hmmm." Westgate dialed my number.

I answered.

"Are you playing tricks on me?" asked Westgate.

"How do you mean?"

"Linking Henry Kissinger to Ahmed Matsalah. Are you setting me up? Is Carlton Price in on this?"

"You're seeing bogeymen," I said. "You can't keep calling me every time there's a new twist or turn that puzzles you."

"What should I do?"

"Don't ask me. You're the FBI director. *You* decide."

"You're not being serious with this book—you're just indulging your . . ."

I hung up.

Westgate farted loudly—a big raspy fart.

"You see! You see!" Westgate hollered to Thompson and Dalkin. "That's not me! That's *him* doing this to me!"

"Who?" said Dalkin, looking around the room. "Henry kiss ass, kiss ass, speck and sauerkraut—oh fuck it!"

Westgate picked up his phone. "Cheryl, I was disconnected. Try Dr. Kissinger again."

Cheryl buzzed two minutes later. "He's in a meeting."

"I don't give a damn! Tell them to interrupt his goddam meeting!" Westgate slammed down the phone. "Can you believe that guy?" Westgate addressed Thompson. "He even puts God on hold."

Westgate sat fuming. So what if he was kissing goodbye to a mid-six-figure job in four years when his term was up? He was the FBI director, goddamit, and he wasn't going to be dicked around by some ex-secretary-of-state who traveled the world consorting with presidents and kings and dictators like he owned them.

Westgate's phone rang. "Dr. Kissinger's office," said Cheryl.

"Please hold for Dr. Kissinger," said Kissinger's secretary, teaching the FBI director a lesson in *Who's Who*.

Five minutes later, Kissinger picked up.

"I'm going to make this short and simple, Henry. Do you have a bank account in Switzerland?"

"None of your business," snapped Kissinger.

"I'm inviting you to Washington tomorrow for a chat with me. If you don't come on your own voli-tion, I'll have you arrested."

"You cannot arrest me." Kissinger could not hide the contempt in his voice. "For what?"

"Extortion."

"Tut, tut."

"I'm serious, Henry."

"Do you know who you're talking to?" Kissinger raised his voice. "Phone my lawyer. James Boggles the Third. He's at Boggles, Boggles and Boggles."

"Henry? Henry? That bastard hung up on me again, goddamit! Do we have a file on him?"

Thompson shrugged.

"Dig up whatever we have on Kissinger. If we're going to arrest him, I'm going to need some leverage."

Thompson picked up a phone and issued instructions to his deputy.

Westgate's phone rang. "It's the president," said Cheryl.

"Oh, shit," Westgate muttered. "Huh? No, I'm sorry Mr. President! That 'oh, shit' wasn't directed at you. It's always a pleasure . . ." Westgate listened. "Yes, I phoned Dr. Kissinger." Westgate listened. "Yes, I know, but . . ." Westgate listened some more. "I have a good reason for . . ."

"It better be the best fucking reason you've ever had for anything in your life!" President Rafferty's bellow could be heard by Thompson and Dalkin. Then he was gone.

Westgate's mood turned foul. And it remained foul until the Bureau's file on Henry Kissinger arrived on his desk two hours later.

Next day. Henry Kissinger was holding court with two of his top associates in a plush Park Avenue office overlooking Park and 52nd Street when Special Agents Newman and Shaw pushed their way into his presence.

A secretary followed the special agents inside, hollering. "I'm sorry, Dr. Kissinger, I couldn't stop these men . . ."

Kissinger remained seated, dignified, and waved her quiet. "It's all right, Helen. Gentlemen, what can I do for you?"

"FBI!" Newman flashed a gold badge. "You're under arrest."

The associates gasped.

"Nonsense," droned Kissinger. "This must be a joke."

The gasps turned to guffaws, in deference to their boss, the great elder statesmen.

"No joke," said Shaw. "Please come with us, sir."

"You dare to barge in on me like this?" droned Kissinger. He turned his attention to his secretary, still standing motionless near the door, wide-eyed, jaw touching the pile carpet. "Helen, get FBI Director Bryant Westgate on the phone immediately."

Kissinger remained seated in a sofa, ignoring the two agents, making small-talk with his associates. A minute later the phone on a small table adjacent to him whistled softly. He picked it up.

"Dr. Kissinger?" said Westgate's secretary. "This

is Cheryl, the director's secretary. He's on a call. Do you mind waiting?"

Kissinger sat, phone to his ear, trying to keep his cool, but fuming nonetheless.

Finally. "Henry?"

"Bryant, I have two men in my private office who burst in purporting to be *special* agents with your Bureau. I do not appreciate this. May I confirm that they belong to you?"

"Yes, I can confirm this."

"You wish to arrest me for something?"

"I would prefer to meet with you privately, Henry. You have two options: One, my agents will take you to the federal building in Manhattan for questioning; or two, you appear in my office at nine sharp tomorrow morning."

"Impossible," barked Kissinger. "I'm flying to India tonight. I have an extremely important meeting with the prime minister."

"I'm afraid not, Henry. I want you to surrender your passport to my agents—that is, if you choose option two."

"This is outrageous," huffed Kissinger. "I'm a former secretary of state." He puffed. "I'm *Henry Kissinger.*"

"Yes, Henry."

"You must have brass balls to think you can treat me this way. When this is over I'm going to hang them on my office wall."

"We'll see. So, is it option two?"

"I will come see you—with my lawyer James Boggles—at nine tomorrow. And you'd better have the attorney general with you. You're going to need him."

"Please put Special Agent Newman on the line."

Kissinger held the phone out to Newman. "Your ill-advised director wishes to speak to you."

Newman took the phone. "Sir?"

"Special Agent Newman. Dr. Kissinger has agreed to surrender himself tomorrow morning. I want you to seize his passport. If he refuses to give it to you, book him."

"Yes, sir. Thank you, sir."

His testosterone level on the rise, Westgate dialed my number.

I answered.

"You realize this is discrimination, don't you?" said Westgate.

"You, again? What the hell are you talking about—discrimination?" I was annoyed. It was Sunday, and my new Compaq Lte Elite had eaten about 750 words for lunch.

"You haven't created *one* female character yet."

"Sure I have—the Legat in Paris, the one who arrived too late to catch Matsalah at the airport."

"Sally Pippin? She had two lines! If you don't have a strong female character, you can't have a sex scene, and if you don't have a sex scene, you don't have a book."

"You're the FBI director. We'll follow Hoover's example."

"No, no, no, no, no—don't even *think* about doing that to me."

"Then stop calling me and do your own job."

"Please think about what I said."

"You just want to get laid, Westgate. Go home and ball your wife if you're looking for gratuitous sex."

"It doesn't have to be for me," said Westgate. "I only have the best interest of your book at heart, Honest."

"If that were true, you wouldn't keep interrupting me."

"See it from my point of view," said Westgate. "It isn't much, but all I've got in the whole world is a role in this book. I just want to make the most of it."

"And get laid," I said.

"Only if it works for the plot!"

"Yeah, right. Tell you what, I'll create a gorgeous blond with great tits."

"Now you're talking."

"She'll meet Dalkin . . ."

"Dalkin? Dalkin's got Tourette's—that's not very romantic!"

"Now look who's discriminating. At least Dalkin looks like Bruce Willis. But you . . ."

"No, don't!"

"Yes, you . . ."

"No!"

". . . You look like Rodney Dangerfield."

"Arghhh!"

"Now leave me alone before I bring Eddie and Junior back from the dead to engage you in a ménage-a-tois."

"You wouldn't."

"Don't be so sure. You've got enough trouble with Carlton Price—and now Henry Kissinger—without pissing me off, too."

7

Henry Kissinger was not in a buoyant mood when he arrived at the J. Edgar Hoover Building on Pennsylvania Avenue. He was accompanied by his lawyer James Boggles the Third, immaculately suited in Saville Row pinstripe and J. Foster handmade brogues.

Inside the director's suite, Westgate and Jim Thompson rose to greet their VIP guest. Kissinger shook hands coldly with the two men and said nothing.

"Please sit down, gentlemen." Westgate gestured to his sofa and three easy chairs around a coffee table.

They sat. Kissinger glared wordlessly at the Bureau chieftains; Boggles sat expressionless, thin lips glued together.

"Henry," began Westgate. "When you served on the President's Foreign Intelligence Advisory Board, you sat in on monthly intelligence briefings, all classified at the highest level, dealing with this nation's most sensitive secrets." It was a statement, not a question.

Kissinger grunted. "Yes."

"And then you habitually used tidbits gleaned from those meetings to solicit new business for Kissinger Associates among foreign leaders and multinational corporations."

Kissinger said nothing, but shifted uneasily in his chair. It was obvious to Westgate that the statesman had been instructed by his lawyer to keep his mouth shut, whatever the temptation to speak.

"Henry," continued Westgate, in a soft tone. "That's treason."

"You'd better be able to prove that!" Boggles erupted staccato-style, like a machine gun.

"I can," said Westgate. "And I will if necessary. I hope it won't be necessary. I would prefer that your client cooperate with the Bureau on another matter."

"My client has a fee schedule for government consulting," shot Boggles. "Ten thousand dollars per day."

"And I'm sure he earns every penny." Westgate smiled. "But I ask that your client waive his fee on this occasion. A trade-off."

Kissinger leaned over and whispered into his lawyer's ear.

"My client is prepared to waive his fee," announced Boggles. "On the basis that the matter with which you desire his cooperation be resolved before lunchtime today."

"Agreed," said Westgate. "Henry, do you have a bank account in Switzerland—a numbered account?"

Kissinger cleared his throat, twisted, and again beckoned his lawyer's ear.

"My client's financial affairs are his own business," said Boggles. "I fail to see . . ."

Westgate raised his hand. "Okay. Let me rephrase this." He turned to Kissinger and held out a piece of paper. "Henry, is this your bank account number?"

Kissinger didn't look. "You are harassing me," he droned.

"Look, Henry, I'm not the IRS—I'm not interested if you're hiding money in numbered accounts to evade taxes"—Westgate filed a mental note to tip off the IRS Commissioner next time they met at the Cosmos Club—"it's just that this account number has surfaced relative to the terrorist attack across the street two weeks ago, and it is also linked to the attack at the Hard Rock Cafe in London last week."

Kissinger sat poker-faced.

"Here," Westgate prodded, "look at these." The FBI director plucked copies of his two Skorpion faxes from a leather portfolio and handed them to Kissinger.

Kissinger read. He paled visibly. Then he spoke slowly, deliberately. "I helped open this account."

"Don't say anything!" Boggles interjected.

Kissinger waved him down. "I had no idea . . . you don't think . . . ?"

Westgate was silent.

Kissinger shook his head vigorously. "Our only involvement at Kissinger Associates with this account was to open it for one of our clients. They asked that the account be in my name. They were prepared to pay for this service. And I saw no reason . . ." Kissinger looked at the faxes. "This is inconceivable."

"Who, Henry?" said Westgate. "Who is the client?"

Kissinger hesitated. But he realized it would be ridiculous to claim client confidentiality under such circumstances. "Faud Hadi Hamade."

"Who is that?"

"A Kurdish leader. He retained my consulting service a year ago to advise him on building a foundation for the establishment of Kurdistan."

"I thought lost causes were St. Jude's domain, Henry?"

"It is unlikely that Turkey and Iraq would ever agree to an independent Kurdish nation," intoned Kissinger, as if he were speaking before the Council on Foreign Relations in New York, "but it is a worthy cause nonetheless. In my opinion the Kurds deserve support."

"What did you *do* for them?"

"Our activities centered on lobbying and gentle education in Washington. Congress, the State Department. Our European friends. We know how to bring attention to their plight, and highlight the reasons they deserve aid. And we opened this account." Kissinger shook his head. "It was a mistake."

"Like Vietnam and Cambodia, Henry?" Westgate couldn't resist.

Kissinger said nothing.

"Did you ever register as a lobbyist for the Kurds?" asked Westgate.

"They aren't a nation."

"A loophole, eh, Henry?"

"Our relationship with them has already been terminated," Kissinger thrummed. "We're still waiting for our bill to be paid. They're now three months overdue and they don't respond to our requests for payment."

Westgate pointed at the faxes Kissinger still held numbly. "They're waiting for a windfall."

"My God," said Kissinger. The full impact of what had transpired—of what he was in the middle of—had finally hit him. "None of this should get out."

"None of it should, but it will," said Westgate. "You're an old pro at failing to plug leaks. I could book you this minute as an accessory to murder— and call a press conference—and I reserve my right to do that. But I'm going to give you the benefit of the doubt, Henry."

"Thank you." It was tough to detect from

Kissinger's drone whether he was speaking sincerely or with sarcasm.

Westgate picked up his intercom phone. "Cheryl? Send Dalkin in."

Kissinger flinched. Already the circle privy to his secret was widening.

Dalkin swaggered into the director's office. The men rose. Westgate greeted Dalkin. Kissinger did a double-take. What the hell was Bruce Willis doing here?

"Jeff, this is Henry Kissinger, and his attorney, James Boggles. Henry, Jeff Dalkin."

Dalkin shook Kissinger's hand. "Kiss ass, kiss ass," said Dalkin, struggling to maintain, but not succeeding. "Speck and sauerkraut."

Kissinger recoiled.

"He has Tourette's," Jim Thompson whispered.

Kissinger nodded, an uncertain nod.

The men sat.

Westgate spoke. "This is the situation, Jeff. Dr. Kissinger opened an account at UBS—the account of interest to us—for a Kurdish leader named . . . Henry?"

"Faud. Faud Hadi Hamade."

Dalkin crouched forward on the edge of his chair, taking mental notes, as Westgate explained the situation.

"It's very simple," said Dalkin. "I should establish a legend as a kiss ass, kiss ass, kiss-kiss-Kissinger—

whew!—Associate and attempt to renew contact with this Kurd. Butt-buggering bastards!"

"Ridiculous." Kissinger dismissed Dalkin's idea with the backhand wave of his hand. "I cannot allow my office to be used for this purpose."

"The way I see it, Henry," said Westgate, "allowing us to use your office is the very *least* you can do to help us resolve this little problem—*your* little problem."

"But if it comes out that I permitted Kissinger Associates to be a front for the FBI," said Kissinger, "my business would be ruined!"

"Less ruined than if I book you right now as an accessory in the murder of over 20 people?"

Kissinger said nothing. The trade-off was clear.

Westgate turned to Dalkin. "There may be a problem to the approach you suggest. This Kurd owes Kissinger Associates money—how much does he owe, Henry?"

"I don't involve myself in invoicing," huffed Kissinger disdainfully.

"C'mon, Henry—how much approximately?"

"I believe it is in excess of half-a-million dollars."

Westgate returned to Dalkin. "The Kurd hasn't paid-up and he's several months overdue. So he may want to avoid any contact with Kissinger Associates."

"Easy," said Dalkin. "My first order of business will be to quash the fee."

"You can't do that!" Kissinger protested.

"Sure I can," said Dalkin. "This will ingratiate myself with him. When you're dealing with a rug merchant, you need something to trade. Butt-buggering bastards. In return for quashing the fee, I'll ask for a favor—and that's what'll get me through his door. Crinkum crankum, pop-a-nut."

"But, but," Kissinger spluttered. "I can't just wipe their debt clean! There were expenses involved!"

"I think, Henry," said Westgate, "you're going to have to tighten your belt and go along with whatever plan we come up with. I must say, Mr. Dalkin's plan sounds damn good. *And* it's all we have."

Boggles leaned toward Kissinger and whispered in his ear. Kissinger nodded.

"We need," Boggles enunciated, "a formal deal in writing that will grant my client full and total immunity from this unfortunate set of circumstances, though we make no admissions as to any guilt."

Westgate's intercom phone rang. He picked up. "Yes?"

"I have Carlton Price on the phone."

"Tell him I'm busy, in a meeting . . ."

"He wants to know if Henry Kissinger is here."

"What?"

"That's what he asked."

"What did you tell him?"

"I said he would have to speak with you."

"Thank you, Cheryl. Put him through. Carlton? Yes, Carlton, I have Dr. Kissinger with me. Uh, no, he's busy—he'll have to call you back." Westgate listened. "Excuse me? Yes, as a matter of fact, that's the issue we're talking about. No, no, don't even think about it—we found him first. Remember, Carlton? May the best man win!"

Westgate gleefully returned the phone to its cradle. "You're right, Henry—about secrets getting out. The CIA already knows about your Swiss account. Carlton Price is shitting his pants because I got to you first."

Boggles turned to Kissinger. "Maybe the CIA will offer us a better deal?"

"Oh, no. It's our deal or *no* deal," said Westgate. "You start playing me off against Price and I'll haul your ass before a grand jury, I don't care how well connected you are."

"What if Carlton phones me," said Kissinger. "We've known each other for years—not that he'd push me into a corner as *you* have. He *values* our relationship."

"You're assisting us on a classified matter. You're not to talk about it outside of this office. Tell him to phone me if he's not satisfied."

"We need to have something concrete in writing," repeated Boggles.

"You're a lawyer," said Westgate. "Draft something and fax it to me this afternoon. I want Dalkin in New York at Kissinger Associates first thing tomorrow morning to study your Faud file—and it had better be untouched when he gets to it. If anything gets shredded, deal's off."

"Boggles, bugles, bagels," added Jeff Dalkin. "Bugger all the fucking lawyers. Speck and sauerkraut."

Westgate's intercom buzzed. "Yes, Cheryl?"

"I have 'the writer' on the phone."

"Who?"

"All he says is 'the writer.' He said you'll know who."

"Okay, put him through."

"It's me," I said.

"Why are you calling me?"

"Oh, it's okay for you to phone me," I said, "spoil *my* rhythm. But it's not okay for me to phone *you*? You just don't get it, do you, Westgate? This is my book, my imagination. And, anyway, it's not you I want to talk to. I want a word with Henry."

"What? Why?"

"What are you, his secretary? Just put Kissinger on the phone and don't be so goddam nosy."

"Why don't you call him at . . ." Westgate farted, a big raspy fart that blew a hole in his underwear. "Goddamit! Quit doing that to me!"

"Kissinger," I said. "I want to talk to him *now*."

"Okay, okay." Blushing purple, Westgate turned to Kissinger. "Telephone for you."

Kissinger ambled over and reluctantly picked up the phone.

"Henry?" I said.

"Yes?" Kissinger droned. "Who is this?"

"This is the writer."

Kissinger covered the mouthpiece and looked sternly at Westgate. "Is this your idea of a joke?"

"No. And I'd be careful if I were you. He's got a lot of control over us—and he plays dirty."

"He has no control over me."

"No? *You* tell him that—see what happens."

"Now see here," Kissinger said into the mouthpiece. "I don't know you. We have nothing to talk about."

Henry Kissinger, excited by an oil painting of a sheep on Westgate's wall, popped a woody. He unzipped his fly and . . .

"Stop! Stop!" yelled Kissinger.

"See?" Westgate smirked.

"What do you want from me!" hollered Kissinger. "You have no right including me in this, this fiction, in the first place. It is an invasion of my privacy!"

"Calm down, Henry," I said. "And button your fly before everybody sees what a small dick you have. You're a public person and therefore I have license to involve you in my plot. I could have written a non-fiction book about you and Kissinger Associates, but this is more fun. I think it is extremely interesting how an ex-secretary-of-state can make millions of dollars using contacts he made while in government service. Do you think that's ethical, Henry?"

"I didn't invent the revolving door. Everybody in Washington does it."

"That doesn't make it right."

"Is that what you called to say?"

"No, that was thrown in spur the moment. The reason I called is to ask if you were 'Deep Throat.' Was it you who sabotaged Nixon?"

"No."

"The truth, Henry."

"That *is* the truth. It wasn't me."

"Do you know who it was?"

"I have a very good idea."

"Who?"

"I can't say." Kissinger let fly a stutter fart: pt, pt, pt-pt, pt-pt-pt, pop, pop-pop, POW. "Okay, okay! It was David Young!"

"Who?"

"David Young. He came from John McCloy. First he worked for me, then Ehrlichman. He was head of the plumbers—Hunt and Liddy reported to him. He knew everything, spilled the beans, then took off to England. He's been there ever since."

"Thank you, Henry. Put Westgate back on."

Kissinger handed the phone to Westgate and zipped his fly. "This," said Kissinger, "is a very strange place."

Westgate took the phone. "What do you want now?" he asked me.

"Don't 'what' me," I said. "Things are going

pretty darn well for you right now. Especially with Carlton Price steamed up about you getting to Kissinger first."

"Is he angry?"

"Very. But this story is about *you*, not *him*, so you have an edge. But that can change, so don't get too cocky."

"What, uh, is Price *doing*?"

"I'm not your spy, Westgate. Hire your own goddam informants."

8

Two weeks after emptying the contents of Jack Hudson's house, a team of burly IRS agents returned. Hudson stood by, watching, as they trudged up his path with couch and chairs, TV and VCR, lamps and beds and rugs and kitchen appliances, and set to putting everything back in its proper place.

So far, the financial tally had come to almost three thousand dollars in hotel bills, meals out and a car rental. The emotional toll for Hudson and his family was much higher. His standing in the neighborhood, and at work, much lower. Neighbors peeked through curtains, snickering.

"Sign here," said a tired, perspiring agent after two hours of hard labor.

"Wait a minute," said Hudson. "Where is my Toyota Camry? And my van?"

The agent scratched his head. "I don't know nothing about motor vehicles."

"Then I suggest you find out." Hudson was irritated. "This form of yours states that all of my belongings have been returned. I'm not signing until I've got *everything* back."

"I just want to go home," said the agent. "Just sign and write that your vehicles ain't here yet."

"No. You get on the phone and find out where my vehicles are and when they're coming."

The agent gritted his teeth and returned to the large van, where three colleagues waited inside. Hudson watched; he could see the agent conduct a discussion on his two-way radio. Then the agent climbed out and lumbered up the path.

"You know your cars were impounded?" said the agent, a cockiness barely disguised by a thin layer of sheepishness.

"Yes?"

"There was a mistake," said the agent. "They auctioned them last week."

"WHAT?"

"Yeah, the highest bidder drove them away." He scratched his head. "Sorry. You'll have to file a claim form." The agent did not sound sorry at all. He handed Hudson his clipboard.

"You're telling me you sold my cars!?"

"Yes, sir, that's correct."

Hudson had returned his rental car that morning and . . .

My phone rang.

"I can't believe this," said FBI Director Westgate.

"It's actually very credible," I said. "Government bureaucracies make mistakes like this all the time—including yours."

"That's not what I meant," said Westgate.

"No?"

"No. Jack Hudson. What's he still doing in this book?"

"Getting his stuff back. I told you already, *I* decide who's in this book."

"But it makes no sense!"

"Look, Westgate, I dragged myself out of bed this morning after a late night and too much wine because I have to write, just like a jogger has to jog, or I feel shitty all day. But I'm sick of you and especially that ugly sucker Kissinger. So, if you don't mind, I'm going to stick with Jack Hudson for a couple of pages."

"I mind! My plot is just starting to take off. I put Kissinger in his place! I'm on a roll!"

"Sorry. But that's the way I feel."

"You, you—it's always the way *you* feel. What about *me*? What about the reader?"

"What about him?"

"Aha! And you accused *me* of being discriminatory! Don't you mean what about *her*? It's a fact that more women read books than men."

"I don't need the FBI to lecture me on discrimination," I said. "Or about books."

"Okay. I take it back. The main thing is, your reader wants *me*, not Hudson.

"You keep talking about the reader. This book belongs to *me*, not the reader."

"But you need readers!"

"Why?"

"What's the point of writing unless a lot of people are going to read what you've written?"

Westgate was starting to grate on my nerves. "I have to write. For myself. No one else. Why do I need a bunch of strangers, people I've never met, reading what I've written? *I* know I've written this! I like reading it! That's all that matters!"

"What about sales," said Westgate. "Money."

"Are you nuts? If this was about money I'd be better off buying a lottery ticket. You know how many books get published every year? You know how many people *buy* them? Please, go away, my head hurts."

"But, but Jack Hudson's just some poor jerk who's been screwed by the IRS. It's a non-story."

"What do you know about stories, Westgate? You think it's okay for a government agency like the IRS to ruin Hudson's life? To sell his cars? I can't just desert him. He deserves vindication. He deserves justice. Tell you what I'll do, I'll cut you a deal: You call the IRS commissioner and get them to replace Hudson's vehicles, cover his expenses and pay him $25,000 for the trouble they've caused him, and I'll consider this episode closed and return to you."

"They'll never do that," said Westgate. "I know how government operates. And you wouldn't dare just make it up, because it isn't credible."

"You think bringing Santos Trafficante back from the dead is credible? I'll do whatever I want. But *you* have to approve and accept the consequences, not me. If the IRS has a problem, screw 'em—your Bureau can put up the bread."

"I can't do that with Bureau funds. It has to be accounted for. The General Services Administration would find it in their next audit and they'd have my balls."

"Oh, c'mon—you mean to tell me your Bureau doesn't have a slush fund of some kind? Drug-bust money?"

"I can't believe this. You're asking for a pay-off to put me back where I belong—at center stage of this book?"

"Not for me. For Jack Hudson. He's been screwed by the government. I'm just asking you to do the right thing—or I'll have to stick with Hudson until he gets justice."

"This is ludicrous."

"No. It's my book. And you're only center stage when I want you to be. Now, I'm sure you've got plenty to do with that mad Kurd on the loose, so if you don't mind . . ."

"And I'd like to do something about that Kurd, but you know damn well I can't do anything until you shove Hudson . . ."

"Exactly. I'm in control. So play ball or take a hike."

"Now you're mixing metaphors."

"Fuck you."

"Okay, okay." Westgate was desperate. "How's this: I'll see to it that Hudson's cars get replaced—I'm sure they'd do that much for him anyway—and get him compensated for expenses. Deal?"

"No. Hudson's status—his whole being—has taken a blow. His nerves are shot. He needs a vacation. Hawaii, maybe. Twenty-five grand should cover it."

"Twenty-five grand for a vacation?"

"Sure. First class, deluxe hotels—look, Westgate, it's not like he doesn't deserve it after what the IRS put him through."

"But *I'm* not the IRS."

"You're government. It's all the same to Hudson."

"Okay, okay. I'll do it."

"Good. Do it now."

"What's the big hurry?"

"Nothing. But I'm going to stick with Hudson until it gets done."

Jack Hudson stormed into his house to phone his lawyer . . .

"No, no!" Westgate was still on my line. "Okay, I'll do it now."

Before Hudson could reach his phone, it rang. He picked up.

"This is FBI Director Bryant Westgate."

"Oh, no—my lawyer said not to talk to you anymore, whoever you really are."

"Whoa, Jack. I really am who I say I am. I know all about your cars getting auctioned."

"You do?"

"Yes. It was a mistake. We're going to replace your cars with brand new ones, straight out of the showroom."

"You are? When?"

"As quickly as possible. Tomorrow. Not only that, but we're going to pick up your expenses—hotel, car rental, everything. Plus . . ."

"Phone my lawyer and make it official," said Hudson.

"Fine. I'll phone him now."

"Yes, Mr. Westgate?" said Bernie Hewitt. "What can I do for you?"

"Your client, Jack Hudson, has been terribly wronged. I'm calling to set the situation straight."

"Go on."

"His vehicles were mistakenly auctioned last week. We're prepared to replace them with new vehicles, even though both were several years old. We are also prepared to meet his expenses for the last couple of weeks: hotel, car rental, meals . . ."

"Excuse me," Hewitt interrupted. "But why is the *FBI* offering a settlement? This is an *IRS* matter, isn't it?"

"Uh, yes, that's correct. But we're, uh, trying to do the right thing, uh, collectively, for your client. We're also going to give your client $25,000 for the trouble he's been caused."

"Why?" Hewitt was suspicious.

"Because we think he deserves it."

"This doesn't have anything to do with you wanting my client—and me—out of this book, does it?"

"What book?"

"Last time you called, you wanted us out of this book, remember?"

"As, yes. You *must* vacate the book, no big deal— I've taken it up with the writer and he agrees. But my offer is . . ."

"Two hundred and fifty thousand dollars," said Hewitt.

"What?"

"My client wants $250,000 punitive damages. That's how much we're going to ask in our suit against the government."

"What suit against the government?"

"I'm already drawing up papers. Not only are

we going to sue, but we're going to do it in *this book.*"

"Impossible."

"You think so? A legal drama is far more compelling than a manhunt. Have you not heard of John Grisham?"

"That's a moot point. This book is not about a legal drama."

"Well, that's where it's going, unless you're willing to settle for a quarter of a million dollars. And I want the assault charge quashed."

"That's extortion."

"Nonsense. You've made an offer, I'm countering."

"The writer has been very generous about wanting to help your client . . ."

"Aha, you see, this *is* about the book."

"He's not going to be happy about your refusal. He may even revoke his offer and write you out completely, and then your client has nothing—he'll spend the next three months filling out forms for the IRS, and then, if he's lucky, they'll give him *book value* on his cars, not new ones like I'm offering."

"Two hundred and fifty thousand dollars," said Hewitt.

"We'll see." Westgate hung up and immediately dialed my number. "Did you catch all that?" he asked me.

"You kidding? I *wrote* it."

"What do you think?"

"He's just doing his job, being a lawyer. Lawyers suck, you know that, Bryant—you used to be one yourself."

9

J eff Dalkin sat alone inside the conference room at Kissinger Associates. Before him, on the highly-polished smooth surface of an oval mahogany table, were spread the contents of the Faud Hadi Hamade file. He read, scribbled notes, grunted. "Speck and sauerkraut."

Outside the room, secretaries tittered in whispers. What was Bruce Willis doing here? Had he become a Kissinger client? Should somebody phone the National Enquirer? It was especially intriguing to them because their autocratic boss, secretive about almost everything, was especially secretive about this particular visitor. And why was he given the name Jeff Dalkin?

Dalkin worked through the morning, took a quick break for lunch, then returned for an afternoon session. Just past four p.m., he stuck his head out of the conference room.

"Is it okay to use the phone in here?"

"Yes," said a secretary, having already been instructed to be helpful to their visitor. "Press nine for an outside line—Bruce."

"Thanks," said Dalkin. "Fuck-fuck-fuck. Yes. Oh boy." Dalkin winked and closed the door behind him. He checked his watch—it was just past ten at night in Switzerland—picked up the phone and touch-keyed a long number.

A phone rang inside Faud Hadi Hamade's heavily fortified villa in Coligny, a hilly, exclusive suburb of Geneva. The Kurd, watching a porn video on his large-screen Grundig TV set, was irritated that his manservant did not answer. He plucked the phone from its cradle after nine rings. Faud said nothing, just listened.

"Hello?" said Dalkin. "Mister Hamade?"

"Who is this?"

"Jeff Dalkin from Kissinger Ass-associates in New York."

"Oh. You must call my office in the morning. I am busy." Hamade assumed this was a harassing reminder call for a payment he had no intention of ever remitting.

"Please, just one minute of your time," said Dalkin.

Hamade seethed, angry at his new manservant for putting him in this most unpleasant predicament and distracting him from the business at hand. And just when he was beginning to grow hard after 30 minutes' concentration. Hamade pressed a remote button to freeze-frame his movie. "Yes, one minute only."

"Thank you, Mister Hamade. As you know, you owe us 679,426 dollars and 36 cents."

Hamade said nothing. He knew this was coming, and he was not about to commit himself in the event that they were recording his words.

"Are you there?" asked Dalkin.

"Yes. Is that all?"

"That's all you *owe*," said Dalkin, "but the reason I'm calling is to say that we're willing to forget about this debt if you'll do us a favor." He put his hand over the mouthpiece in time. "Cocksucking Kurds!"

"What favor?" Hamade was intrigued. He could bill his organization for the amount owed Kissinger Associates and bank it himself.

"It's very sensitive," said Dalkin. "I need to see you in person."

Hamade sighed and looked down. By now he had lost any semblance of an erection. "You will come to Geneva?"

"Yes. I could catch a flight tonight and see you tomorrow."

"Yes. Come. Call my office when you arrive." Hamade put the phone down. He thought a moment, then flipped through an address book. He picked up the phone and dialed.

lobby, leaving instructions with the hotel operator to page him.

Dalkin took a seat at the far end of the contemporary lobby and ordered *cafe au lait*. From a distance, he thought he saw Claudia Schiffer, the German model, perusing the fine watches and pens displayed at the exclusive boutiques buffering the lobby from the street outside. She drew closer, glancing at him. Dalkin was used to this—another Bruce Willis fan. Then she approached.

"May I sit down?" she asked.

"I'm not Bruce Willis," said Dalkin. "Pop-a-nut."

"And I'm not Claudia Schiffer."

"How . . . ?" Dalkin was confused by this mindreader.

"I'm often told I look like Claudia Schiffer."

"Then grab a seat—I guess we're a good match." Dalkin paused, trying desperately to swallow it back. "Pubic pussy."

Bryant Westgate dialed my number.

"What?" I said plaintively.

"You knew it was me?"

"Of course."

"I don't think . . ."

"You don't think what?" I snapped. "You don't think Dalkin should get the girl, right?"

"A Claudia Schiffer look-alike? And he's already cussing at her!"

"He can't help it. And that's not what this is about. You're just jealous. You think you're the star of this book. First you don't want Hudson around. And now you want Dalkin out of the limelight. You're a goddam book hog, that's what you are. You keep butting in . . ."

"But, but . . ."

"See! You want center stage? You want gratuitous sex? You got it, buster!"

At the very moment Westgate put down his phone, Cheryl stepped into his office and closed the door behind her.

"Cheryl?" Westgate was puzzled, unaccustomed to this kind of intrusion by his secretary without notice or invitation.

"Bryant, I can't stand it anymore!" Cheryl loosened her skirt and let it drop to her ankles, exposing black lace stockings, garter belt and no panties. "Take me, Bryant! Take me on your desk!"

Westgate stood frozen.

Cheryl licked her lips sensuously as she unbuttoned her blouse and let it fall to the floor, then unsnapped her bra.

Westgate reached for the phone and, frantically, began to dial my number. Cheryl rushed him. With one hand, she disconnected the phone; with the other, she expertly unzipped his fly and groped for his dick, in there somewhere.

"Where is it?" she asked.

This scenario was not exactly Westgate's fantasy, but he was aroused by now, even if Cheryl weighed 206 pounds and had the face of a prize hog. She sat on the edge of his desk and spread her legs.

"Ball me, Bryant! Ball me!"

Westgate lunged forth and penetrated Cheryl. In and out, in and out, pumping away.

"Is it in yet?" asked Cheryl.

Twenty seconds later it was all over.

Cheryl tried her conceal her disappointment. She plucked her skirt from the carpet and waddled to Westgate's executive washroom.

Bryant zippered his fly and sat in his swivel chair, confused, humiliated, pissed-off.

Dalkin looked into the clear blue eyes of his new acquaintance. "You are American . . ."

"Call me Claudia." Her eyes twinkled. "And I'll call you Bruce. Yes. I'm From Washington."

"DC?"

"No. Washington State. Outside of Seattle."

"Are you staying in the hotel?"

"No," Claudia shook her head. "I have an apartment in Geneva. And you?"

"Yes. I'm here on business. Pop-a-nut."

"What do you do?"

"I'm a private consultant."

"What kind of consulting? For whom?"

"That's the private part."

The concierge bounded over to Dalkin and leaned over. "Mr. Dalkin?" he inquired softly. "Telephone."

"Excuse me, Claudia," said Dalkin. "I'll be right back."

Dalkin followed the concierge to his desk and picked up the phone.

"Mr. Dalkin? This is Faud Hadi Hamade. You come tonight?"

"Where?"

"My villa in Coligny. Ten o'clock. We talk. You know how to find?"

"Yes, I have the address."

Faud was gone. Dalkin returned to Claudia.

"Who was that?" she asked.

"A business associate," said Dalkin. "Cocksucking Kurds! I'm sorry, I . . ."

"No, it's okay. Consulting for a Kurd?"

"Butt-buggering bastards! Yes, consulting. What do you do?"

"Actually, Bruce, I work for the CIA." Claudia paused, allowing her statement to sink in.

Dalkin cracked a half-smile and cocked an eyebrow, looking more like Bruce Willis than Bruce Willis. "Really?"

"Really. We've been tapping Faud Hadi Hamade's telephones. We have an interest in him and we're hoping that you might help us."

"Nothing like getting to the point," said Dalkin.
"Why should I help you?"

"Patriotism?"

"I don't need the CIA—cunt farts—to test my
patriotism."

"Okay." Claudia smiled. "Then money."

"How much?"

"It depends."

"On what?"

"On what happens."

"What's *supposed* to happen?"

"You tell me," said Claudia. "You're the high-
priced consultant."

"How do you know I'm high-priced? Whoremongering mutherfuckers!"

"There's no such thing as a low price at Kissinger
Associates."

"Kiss ass, kiss ass," spat Dalkin. "Speck and sauerkraut. Sturimo stoots."

"Excuse me?"

Dalkin blushed. "I have Tourette's," he mumbled.
"Haven't you noticed?"

"You have *what*?"

"Tourette's. Tourette syndrome. Blow me."

"Oh." Claudia wasn't exactly sure what this meant.

"I'd like to think about your proposal," said
Dalkin. "I'd like to fuck your hairy cunt—No! I'm
sorry! I didn't mean that!"

"Okay," said Claudia, studying Dalkin suspiciously. "Think about it. And tell me your answer over dinner this evening. Do you like Chinese?"

"Sure."

"There's an excellent Chinese restaurant in this hotel." Claudia pointed to the nearby elevator bank. "Upstairs. It's called Yang-Tse. Seven o'clock?"

"Fine. Yang-Tse. Yank me."

Inside his room, Jeff Dalkin picked up his phone, paused a moment, and returned it to its cradle. He went downstairs, purchased a phone-card from the concierge and found a public phone. He dialed Jim Thompson's direct line at FBI headquarters. Thompson answered.

"It's Dalkin. I just had an interesting encounter with someone from the Agency. Cunt-farts."

"What?"

"They're onto our Kurd. They're tapping his phone. And they think I'm a kiss ass, kiss ass—you know, kiss ass—oh, fuck it! They want me to help *them*."

"For chrissakes . . . What did you tell him?"

"*Her*. I said I'd think about it. She's wining and dining me tonight."

"Hold on. I'm going to connect the director."

"Carlton fucking Price!" hollered Westgate, joining the conversation.

"I've got Dalkin here," said Thompson. "Dalkin, you still there?"

"Yes, sir."

"Director Westgate is on the line."

"So I hear. He sounds like me."

"This isn't a bad situation, Bryant," Thompson consoled. "It's actually a blessing. We couldn't have *planned* something this good. Dalkin can feed the Agency *disinformation*."

"Hmmm," said Westgate. "So you want Dalkin to stay in contact with the Agency's operative?"

"Exactly. He should accept her offer, then feed her leads that divert them away from the real action."

"That okay with you, Dalkin?" asked Westgate.

"You're the boss," said Dalkin. "Big bossy butt-head. Sorry . . ."

"Just do it," said Westgate, annoyed. "And keep me posted, Jim."

Westgate immediately dialed my number. I answered.

"Don't let that foul-mouthed spastic sleep with her!" Westgate exploded.

"Who?"

"Dalkin. Don't let him sleep with her—that Claudia Schiffer look-alike—she's CIA."

"I know. You're just jealous."

"Seduction and pillow talk are typical CIA tactics."

"Bollocks. Rather than phoning me constantly and concerning yourself with whatever nookie Dalkin may or may not get, you'd be better off looking after your own skin. This Dalkin pick-up is not the only thing Carlton Price is up to."

"Really? What else is he doing?"

"I don't know myself, because I haven't given it much thought yet. But let's not delude ourselves. The CIA is better at overseas operations than you are. And while you're screwing your fat, ugly secretary, Price is undoubtedly mobilizing his stations in Geneva, London, Paris and Istanbul.

"Uh, you won't let that episode with my secretary out of the bag, will you?"

"I haven't decided. It was awfully funny."

"No, c'mon. It wasn't even *me*. It was *you!*"

"You think anyone's going to buy that?"

Claudia—real name Tamara Burnham—was sitting at Yang-Tse's small bar when Jeff Dalkin arrived.

"Something to drink, Bruce?"

"You buying, Claudia?"

"It's on Uncle Sam tonight."

"Gin and tonic."

"Let's sit down," said Tamara. "They'll bring it to the table."

A maitre d' led the pair to a table for two next to a picture window overlooking Lake Lemann. In the distance, the jet d'eau ejaculated into a light breeze, spraying the young dope-smokers on the quai below.

"Do you mind if I order for us?" asked Tamara.

"Please do." Dalkin was amused by Tamara's take-control tactics.

"We'll start with steamed chicken dumplings, two orders," she addressed the waiter. "And hot sake."

The waiter scribbled and scrambled.

"Have you considered my proposal?" Tamara's eyes pierced Dalkin's.

"Yes."

"And?"

"You know, we have a policy against this sort of thing at kiss ass, kiss ass, kiss ass—you know who I mean. Speck and sauerkraut."

"Of course you do."

"Why are you so interested in our Kurdish client? Butt-buggering bastards!"

"We try to keep up to date on what's going on in the world," Tamara winked. "Including what the Kurds are doing."

Dalkin chuckled to himself. Claudia wasn't planning a two-way street with Bruce.

"You couldn't be asking me to stick my neck out for mundane information collection?"

"Umm, there's more to it than that." Tamara shifted in her chair. "I can't go into details—at least not yet."

"Okay." Dalkin put up his hands and smiled. "I don't want you to tell me anything classified."

"I wouldn't," said Tamara.

"You mentioned payment," said Dalkin.

"Yes. I'm authorized to pay for services rendered."

"You realize that if I got found out, I'd lose my job at kiss ass, kiss ass, speck and sauerkraut. Nems." Dalkin added this last word to his Tourettic repertoire—the French word for egg rolls.

"I appreciate that."

"I earn a high salary, benefits, insurance, nems. All that would go. Nems."

"Um-hm." Tamara was being set up for a high price and she knew it.

"I really couldn't do this for less than a hundred thousand dollars."

Tamara blinked. She'd been authorized to pay well, if absolutely necessary, but not *that* well. "Oh my goodness," she said. "We're not even in the same ballpark."

"We can still have a nice dinner," said Dalkin, poker-faced.

Steamed chicken dumplings arrived. Dalkin lifted one to his mouth with chopsticks. It was succulent, tasty, arousing. "Good choice," said Dalkin.

Unbeknownst to them both, a man outside, on the quai, was pointing a camera equipped with a telephoto-lens in their direction and madly snapping his shutter release.

Tamara swallowed the last of her eight, bite-size dumplings. "I have to make a call."

She got up and made her way down to the Noga-Hilton's lobby and a public phone. She press-keyed the direct line of her chief, working late at Geneva station.

"Nesbit."

"Don, it's Tamara. He wants a hundred thousand dollars."

"He's dreaming."

"No. He says there's too much at stake—it's not worth his while unless he makes out big."

"Offer him fifty. He'll take it. Everybody needs money, no matter how much they earn."

"Yes, chief. And if he doesn't take it?"

"I'll phone headquarters. This guy seems to be important to them."

Burnham returned to Dalkin's table. He looked up at her and smiled pleasantly. She sat down.

"I've been authorized," said Tamara, "to offer you $50,000."

"Cash?"

"Yes."

"All right . . ."

Tamara smiled.

"We'll split the difference," Dalkin continued. "Seventy-five thousand."

"I don't think . . ."

"Take it or leave it. Are we having a main course, Claudia?"

"Uh, yes." Tamara summoned a waitress and ordered Chicken Yang-Tse, one sweet and sour shrimp dish, mixed noodles and *riz nature*.

The waitress scribbled, disappeared and reappeared with hot sake. She poured the clear rice wine and set it into a bucket of steaming hot water.

"What makes you think Faud Hamade is worth so much to us?" asked Tamara.

"I've never given it any thought," Dalkin replied. "The price has to do with me, not him. Cocksucking camel-copulating Kurdish ka-kas!"

"Oh."

"You tell me." Dalkin took a swig of sake and felt its warmth descend his gullet. "Why is he worth so much?"

"You're seeing him tonight?" said Tamara.

Dalkin checked his watch. "Very soon tonight."

"Excellent! We can defer this discussion till tomorrow and then we'll know what we're talking about."

"Speck and sauerkraut," said Dalkin. "Nems."

10

Jeff Dalkin stood waiting for a taxi outside the Noga-Hilton's front entrance. A man wearing a trenchcoat approached.

"Excuse me, Bruce, was that Claudia Schiffer you were dining with?"

"I'm not Bruce Willis," said Dalkin. "Crinkum crankum, pop-a-nut."

"Incognito are we?"

"What's it to you?"

"I'm a reporter with the *National Enquirer*."

"You're making a mistake. Willie Wanker whacking his wong. Nems."

"Oi? I don't think so, mate."

"Buzz off."

A Mercedes taxi rolled up. Dalkin jumped in. He showed the driver an address in Coligny; the cabbie grunted and hit the gas pedal. A right-turn on Quai du Mont Blanc, a left over the Mont Blanc

Bridge, then left out of Geneva. Dalkin did not notice that the *National Enquirer* was in hot pursuit.

The cabbie stopped on a quiet street, beneath a pair of ten-foot high gates. Dalkin handed him a fifty-franc note and alighted. He pressed an entry button on a cement post adjacent to the gate. The area was immediately lit with bright light for the benefit of security guards monitoring a closed-circuit TV system.

"Mr. Dalkin?" A gravelly voice reached out to Dalkin through an intercom.

"Yes."

"Please come in."

The gates opened electronically. Dalkin walked a lighted path as it meandered through immaculately landscaped gardens. The villa, first shielded by trees, now appeared before him. Stark, stucco, square-shaped; ochre-colored; quiet and austere.

Two bodyguards at the front door gestured that Dalkin should raise his arms. He did so and they wordlessly patted him down, feeling for weapons. They found nothing unusual and let him pass.

Faud Hadi Hamade, clad in a colorful Sulka silk robe, stood in a grand foyer decorated with statues in cream-colored marble of nude boys. "Welcome to my villa, Mr. Dalkin. Come."

Dalkin followed the Kurd into a wood-paneled library.

"You like?" asked Hamade. He didn't wait for

an answer. "All imported from England—from a men's club on Pall Mall. A drink?"

Hamade opened a cabinet that housed a spectacular display of single-malt scotch whiskies. "May I suggest a 25 year-old Macallan?"

Dalkin nodded appreciatively.

Hamade uncapped a fresh bottle and poured the rust-colored whiskey into two tumblers. "The color deepens with age," said Hamade. He handed Dalkin a tumbler. "To your good health." He raised his glass and sipped. "You have friends outside?"

"Excuse me?"

"Two men in a car. They are with you, no?"

"That's news to me. I came here alone. Cuntfarts." Dalkin steamed inside. Goddam CIA!

"They follow you maybe?"

"It's possible." Their likely identities suddenly dawned on Dalkin. The *National Enquirer*. Of course—Claudia would not be so indiscreet. "I think they may be reporters for a tabloid newspaper."

"Reporters? Why?"

"They think I'm Bruce Willis. Crinkum crankum, pop-a-nut."

"Ah. Yes, I do see a similarity. How long have you been with Kissinger Associates?"

"Kiss ass, kiss ass," said Dalkin. "Speck and sauerkraut. Nems. Not long."

Hamade narrowed his eyes, trying to fathom Dalkin's handicap.

"What can I do for you?" he asked.

"You owe kiss ass, kiss ass—oh, shit!—you owe us $679,426."

"But you have come to cancel this debt, no?" said Hamade. "This is why I invite you into my home."

"Actually, I just said that to get into your home."

Faud's thick black eyebrow narrowed over his large, hawk-shaped nose. "For what reason?"

"Blackmail." Dalkin was nonchalant.

"What?"

"Those attacks in Washington and London—I've traced them to the account we opened for you in Zurich. Whoremongering Swiss."

"Henry wants to blackmail me?" Faud spat contemptuously.

"No. Henry doesn't know. Your account was given to me and I figured it out myself. I want a piece of the action."

"I could have you killed like this." Hamade snapped his fingers. "And drop your corpse like a stone to the bottom of Lake Geneva."

"This isn't Kurdistan," said Dalkin. "Nothing like that happens here, and you like living in Switzerland too much to take that kind of risk. In any case, my brother knows I'm here. He has a key to a safe deposit box that has a copy of my file on you. If I do not return, his instructions are to retrieve this file and give it to the FBI."

"Kissinger Associates," said a female voice.

"I wish to speak with Jeff Dalkin," said Hamade.

"I'll connect you," said the voice.

Satisfied, Hamade put the receiver down and pushed a button to rewind his video and start over. It took him another hour, but Faud finally achieved a hard-on. Now he readied himself to be presented with a 12 year-old Kurdish boy, selected this night for the honor of a brutal buggering by Faud Hadi Hamade.

Jeff Dalkin stood at Swissair's check-in line at JFK for the evening nonstop to Geneva. Two teen-agers stood nearby, giggling, ogling him. One stepped toward him shyly.

"Excuse me, Mr. Willis—could I have your auto-graph?"

"Crinkum crankum, pop-a-nut," said Dalkin. "Speck and sauerkraut."

The two girls fled in horror. Dalkin shrugged and checked in for his flight.

Ten hours and 3,500 miles later, Dalkin settled into a fourth-floor room with partial lake view in the Noga-Hilton. He unpacked, showered, and phoned Faud Hadi Hamade's office number. Faud's personal assistant took his name and number.

Dalkin ordered a room service lunch so as not to miss Hamade's call. But, hours later, and no call back, he wished a change of scenery and went down to the

11

Ahmed Matsalah drained an espresso in the Cafe du Midi and strolled out into the early morning sunshine in Tourettes-sur Loup, an inland village on the French Riviera. He checked his watch: 7:15 a.m. Matsalah climbed into a Renault 5, which he had rented at Nice-Cote d'Azur Airport six days before, and drove out of Tourettes, through Vence, to a public bus depot two kilometers from the quiet French town. This is where a schoolbus for the American International School made its last pick-up before continuing down the mountain into Nice.

Matsalah sat inside his vehicle, watching as parents dropped their children at the depot—children aged from six to seventeen. At ten-past-eight precisely, the large blue and white bus, coming from Vence, slowed and careened to a halt in the depot's forecourt. Its door folded open and the children filed up into the bus, gleefully joining their friends who had been collected from other locations throughout a ten-mile-square region in the Alps Maritimes.

Matsalah casually climbed out of his Renault and strolled over to the bus. The French bus driver, mistaking Matsalah for a parent, waved, smiled and mouthed "*bonjour*." After the last child entered the bus, Matsalah stepped up. He reached beneath his windbreaker and from his waistband pulled a Skorpion VZ 61. He pointed the weapon at the bus driver. The driver, mortified, put up his hands. Ahmed was not taking hostages. He pulled the trigger mechanically and pumped six shots into the driver's torso. With a muscular right arm, Matsalah reached beneath the driver's armpit and hauled him out of his seat, across the platform and through the door. The driver landed in a puddle of blood and lay crumpled and dead on the street.

Matsalah turned to the children. They stared back at him in shock. A teenage boy stood up and swore at Matsalah. With one hand, the Kurd swung his weapon and fired on automatic. The impact of the bullets at short range picked the boy up and flung him ten feet down the aisle. The children screamed and cowered beneath the seats in front of them.

Silently, Matsalah positioned himself behind the wheel. The engine was still running. He released the brake and planted his foot on the gas pedal. The bus accelerated with a screech and weaved into the road, heading downhill. Matsalah checked his rearview mirror. About 30 children bobbed in their seats, clutching each other silently.

Matsalah drove on, coming to terms with the bus's weight and power. He slowed, straining his neck, looking for the right spot. He had not had time to properly research this operation, to survey the topography.

But there it was, in the distance—a curve, over which bordered a sheer drop into a craggy, deep ravine. Matsalah slowed the vehicle and hit the switch that opened the accordion door. He steadied the steering wheel, gave the gas pedal one final thrust with his right foot and bailed out.

Matsalah curled up into a ball and rolled out his impact with the gravelly road. Beyond him, the large bus burst through an ineffectual road barrier and disappeared over the edge. Matsalah was captivated by the faces of two young children who watched him from the back window of the bus, their eyes wide with horror as the bus tipped over the edge.

Matsalah picked himself up, brushed the dirt from his dark trousers and limped to a moped, which he had hidden beneath some brush earlier that morning. Another minute later, he was put-puttering down the mountain road into the outskirts of Nice.

By the time the first rescue squads had reached the scene, Matsalah was inside Terminal Two at Nice

Airport, holding a ticket for an Air Inter flight to Strasbourg.

Would-be rescuers found no one to rescue. The vehicle's fuel tank had ignited on impact, leaving only the skeleton of a smoldering, blackened bus. They found charred textbooks and notebooks and children's limbs. They would eventually find a Skorpion VZ 61.

The American International School, 10 miles away, evolved spontaneously into a crisis center as hysterical parents began arriving in search of their sons and daughters, not knowing which of four busses had met with disaster.

The first newsmen on the scene reported a terrible crash. Jeff Dalkin knew better. Watching the reports on CNN in his Geneva hotel room, his stomach turned inside-out.

Bryant Westgate was awakened at four a.m. by a Bureau duty officer. The FBI Director hurried to his office, arriving just past five. A fax awaited him:

> This was only sorbet in between courses. We continue to await your payment, which has now accrued interest. Please wire $525 million today.
>
> Skorpion

Westgate, incredulous, summoned Jim Thompson, who had also been awakened at home and was now at headquarters. The two men sat in the director's office, watching the action on CNN. Video footage from a helicopter showed the unspeakable devastation. A reporter confirmed that 28 children had been aboard the schoolbus—17 American, five British, three French, two Italian and a Swede. No names were yet released, pending the notification of parents. A correspondent excitedly announced that the bus driver was found shot to death in the street three miles away. The French police were now calling the disaster area a crime scene.

The picture switched to the American International School, where parents were seen huddled, crying, embracing each other.

"What kind of monster would do this?" wailed one distraught mother of two missing children.

Ahmed Matsalah climbed into a taxi at Strasbourg Airport.

"Le Gare," he told the cabbie.

Matsalah alighted and purchased a one-way ticket to Geneva.

Somehow or other, the Arab-American Institute had gotten wind of this manuscript and tracked me down. The caller identified himself as its president James Zogby.

"You realize that you are giving Arabs a bad name," he said.

"Yes," I replied. "I realize this."

"It's not fair, this stereotyping."

"It's *my* book," I said. "Don't buy it—I don't care. It's not my fault if Arab genetics are compelled to blow people away on religious grounds."

"You see, you see! This is just what I mean. The great majority of Arabs do not 'blow people away.'"

"Yeah, but the ones who *do* get up my nose. And so do the Kurds in my book, emphasis on *my*. If you want to make a case, call Bryant Humble at the Today show—they like this kind of thing. Or hire Johnny Cockroach, uh, Cochran and sue me. Or get that costive old curmudgeon Jonathan Yardley to skewer me in the *Washington Post*. I don't care."

I really didn't.

I put the phone down and considered shelving this manuscript altogether. It was getting just too weird.

Then Bryant Westgate was on the line, begging me to continue.

"We're getting close to resolving this thing," he pleaded "Carlton Price is going to eat shit."

"Just because you know that Faud Hadi Hamade is your culprit doesn't mean you can get him," I cautioned.

"We'll see." Westgate exuded confidence. "I'm on extremely good terms with my counterpart in

Switzerland. When he hears what we have on Faud, they'll turn him over."

"If you say so."

I wasn't so sure.

People throughout the United States tuned into CNN's "Breaking News"—special live reporting from the Cote d'Azur. Citing unnamed senior officials in the Justice Department, newsmen were now linking the schoolbus attack to those on Au Bon Pain in Washington and the Hard Rock Cafe in London.

Bernie Hewitt was watching CNN in his West Long Branch, New Jersey office when Jack Hudson arrived for a nine a.m. meeting.

"Sit down, Jack." Bernie gestured to a seat facing his desk.

"The FBI has offered $25,000, plus immediate replacement of your cars, plus your hotel and food expenses. In return, they want you to leave this book."

"Jeez!" Hudson's eyes widened. "Take it!"

"I think there's room for negotiation here." Hewitt rubbed his hands together. "The FBI director wants us out of this book very badly. I think he's prepared to go much higher if we stick it out."

"But what if he doesn't?" said Hudson. "And what if he withdraws his offer? I could use 25 grand! I didn't want to be in this book in the first place."

"Of course not. This experience was awful for

you—all the more reason to make them pay out their nose."

"Yeah, I guess I see your point."

"This FBI director has inadvertently *strengthened* our role in the book. His offer makes good reading. We'd be crazy to get out now."

The thought did pass through Hudson's mind that maybe Hewitt was taking personal advantage of this unique situation. After all, it was Hudson's predicament with the IRS that had gotten him in this book, not Hewitt.

"I can get us at least fifty grand," said Hewitt. "I feel it in my bones."

"Fifty-thousand dollars?" Hudson's eyes widened.

"Yes. On the basis that we split fifty-fifty anything over 25 thousand."

"And what if we get nothing?"

"If they revoke their offer—and they won't— I'll represent you in a major suit against the government that'll cost you nothing because I'll do it on a contingency basis. In effect, we take over this book."

Director Westgate dialed my number. He was furious.

"You see what those guys are up to?" he exploded. "They're not worthy!"

"It's not Hudson," I said. "It's the lawyer. He can't help himself."

"You've got to dump them. No money. It's their own fault for being greedy."

"Dammit, Westgate. Twenty-eight children were just murdered by a terrorist and you're worried about Jack Hudson? Go back to work—or I'm quitting this book and going out for a beer."

Westgate put down the phone and buzzed Cheryl.

"Yes, Bryant—I mean, Mr. Westgate. Do you want me to come in?"

"No! Get me Roland Zimmerman in Berne—a secure phone."

"Yes, sir."

Within a minute, Westgate was connected.

"I need a favor, Roland."

Westgate briefed his Swiss counterpart, who listened impassively.

Five minutes later the FBI Director was spent, his case for extraditing Faud Hadi Hamade laid out.

"No." Roland said this quietly with firmness.

"No? But why?"

"You would have to use Faud Hamade's numbered Swiss account as evidence in court. Your case is based on this. We cannot have our banking secrecy violated in this way. Our economy depends on it."

"This Kurd was directly responsible for the murder of 28 children!" shrilled Westgate.

"I'm sorry," said Roland.

Westgate put down the phone and looked at Jim Thompson. "He's *sorry*."

"I think I know how we can do this," said Thompson.

"How?"

Thompson laid out his plan.

12

"Yes, okay." Dalkin listened to Thompson's plan over the phone. "Uh-huh, yeah, got it. Speck and sauerkraut. Nems."

Dalkin put down the phone, removed then reinserted his telecom card and dialed a second number.

"Political Liaison," said a female voice.

"It's me. Dalkin."

"Oh, hello." This was Tamara Burnham. "I tried to call you at . . ."

"I checked out."

"So I heard. Are you still in Geneva?"

"Yes."

"Shall we meet?"

"Do you have money for me?" asked Dalkin.

"How much?"

"All of it. Seventy-five thousand."

"First I'd like to hear what happened last night."

"No, Claudia. I've got nothing to say until I pocket some cash. Pimps and whores."

"Hold on." Tamara covered the mouthpiece with her hand and conversed with others in her office for about a minute. "I can muster $15,000 now. The rest will come . . ."

"Uh-uh," said Dalkin. "Twenty-five down."

"Hold on." Thirty seconds passed. "Okay. Twenty-five thousand."

"Meet me in St-Jean," said Dalkin.

"Where?"

"It's a suburb west of Geneva. You'll see a patisserie with a tea-room in back. I'll meet you in 30 minutes."

At 4:30 p.m. Dalkin sat in a corner of the small tea-room, his back to the wall. Tamara Burnham arrived soon after. She sat across from Dalkin.

"Did you bring the money?"

"Yes." She passed a plastic carrier bag across the table.

Dalkin opened the bag and peeked inside. Switzerland was the best place in the world for fast cash.

"Faud is the guy you're looking for."

"How do you know we're looking for someone?"

"You know what I mean. Faud is the man behind the terrorist attack this morning outside of Vence. Butt-buggering bastards! Fuck-fuck-fuck—yes, oh-boy! Stoots. Stoots McGoots. Godammit! That's why you're so interested in him."

"How can you be sure?"

Dalkin smirked and sipped hot tea. "Simple. I'm blackmailing him." Dalkin pulled a tiny micro-cassette recorder from inside his jacket pocket. "Listen. This was last night." He pressed play:

Faud: "Oh, they'll pay."

Dalkin: "What makes you so sure?"

Faud: "You'll see tomorrow."

Dalkin: "What's so special about tomorrow?"

Faud: "I am serving another course. Five hundred million is nothing to America."

Dalkin pressed stop.

Burnham stirred in her chair. "May I have this tape." She attempted nonchalance.

"Sure. After I receive the other fifty thousand. But the more important question before us is, do you want to apprehend him? Blow me. Nems."

"That's for headquarters to decide."

"Find out," said Dalkin. "We can do it."

"Where?"

"We have to get him out of Switzerland—across the border into Germany."

"Will he go?"

"Not on his own. We have to give him some help."

"What kind of help?"

Dalkin outlined his plan. The CIA case officer took careful notes.

"Do you have a deadline on this?" asked Tamara. "A week or two?"

"Two hours," said Dalkin.

"I don't think ..."

"It's tonight or never."

"I'd better get back to the office. Where are you staying?"

"I'll phone *you*," said Dalkin. "In two hours. And remember, fifty thousand—this evening. You leave first. I'll stay here for five minutes. Crinkum-crankum, pop-a-nut. Nems."

"Were you in the CIA before you joined Kissinger Associates, Bruce?"

Dalkin smiled, a crooked Bruce Willis smile.

From a public phone on Avenue St-Jean, Dalkin touch-keyed a number. He was told that Faud Hamadi was on another line, could he leave a number?

"No, I'm in transit. I'll hold."

"I don't know how long ..."

"I don't care," said Dalkin. "Interrupt him, tell him it's Jeff Dalkin, I'm holding."

Two minutes later Faud was on the line. "Ah, Mr. Dalkin. I have been expecting your call." Faud paused. Dalkin remained silent. "We have decided to accept your proposal. This, of course, is based on our prompt receipt of funds. I am hopeful they will arrive soon." Faud chuckled.

"Let's have dinner tonight," said Dalkin. "We'll firm things up."

"I'm busy," said Hamadi. "I have an important visitor."

"So, we'll make it a party."

"Why not," Hamadi laughed. He was feeling buoyant this day. "*You* join *us*. Le Cheval Blanc. Do you know it? It's outside of Geneva, in . . ."

"I'll find it."

"Good. Eight o'clock."

At seven p.m. precisely Dalkin phoned Tamara Burnham.

"Claudia? Bruce."

"We're on, Bruce," said Tamara. "Just one thing—I need your social security number and date of . . ."

"Blow me," said Dalkin. "And that wasn't Tourettes."

"It's normal procedure."

"This isn't a normal situation."

"No. But headquarters . . ."

"I don't care about headquarters. Clap shack. If you're on, find a commercial moving van and park outside Le Cheval Blanc at nine o'clock tonight. Bring a couple of goons with you. And bring the money. All of it."

"What then?"

"I'll tell you at nine-o-five." Dalkin put the phone down.

Dalkin climbed into a taxi at a rank up the street from the Hotel Bristol. Twenty minutes later the cabbie deposited him in front of Le Cheval Blanc—set in a quiet village—the best restaurant in the Geneva-area.

Dalkin entered, looked around, and admired the fine oil paintings that hung on the wall. A maitre d' confronted him.

"Mr. Hamade is expecting me," said Dalkin.

"Ah, yes. He has no arrived. I take you to table, Mr. Willis?"

"I'm not . . . oh, never mind. Crinkum crankum."

The maitre d' led Dalkin through a front room, into another, past a trolley of cream pastries concocted in heaven. Deeper into the multi-room restaurant, to a corner table. Dalkin sat and studied the menu given him.

Minutes later, Faud Hadi Hamade appeared with two swarthy young men. One looked around the room, then gestured Faud and the other man through.

Dalkin stood up. Faud sauntered over.

"This is Ahmed Matsalah." Faud introduced the swarthy young man.

Jeff Dalkin had managed to restrain his syndrome till now; had limited his copralia and echolalia to kiss ass, kiss ass, speck and sauerkraut, and the occasional nems and sturimo stootz. Now, faced with the man who had massacred a bunch of FBI employees, assassinated the CIA's London station chief along with his secretary and many innocents at the Hard Rock Cafe, and had slaughtered 28 school children that very day, Dalkin could no longer control himself.

"Fuck-fuck-fuck-fuck-fuck-fuck-fuck-fuck-fuck-fuck-fuck-fuck-fuck! FUCK! SHIT! Oh, SHIT! FUCKING CUNT-FACED BUTT-BUGGERING BRAIN-FARTS! WHOREMONGERING MUTHER-FUCKING CAMEL-HUMPING PILE OF SHIT, PISS AND PIG PUKE!"

The maitre d' came running. The waiters froze. Other diners gasped. Faud looked around in horror. Ahmed Matsalah backed off.

"I'm sorry!" Dalkin was purple with embarrassment. He threw his head back to crack his neck, then thrust it up like a jack-in-the-box. "I have Tourette's. Uh-oh, here it comes again. FUCK! FUCK! FUCK YOU! FUCK YOUR OWN FUCKING ASSHOLES, YOU WHOREMONGERING CUNTFARTING COCKSUCKING MUTHERFUCKS!"

The maitre d' tried to shush Dalkin with hand gestures.

"I have Tourette's syndrome," wailed Dalkin. "I can't help myself!"

"This is," Faud started again, shaken. "Ahmed Matsalah."

Dalkin shook hands with Matsalah, silently, avoid-

ing the eye contact that might hasten another outburst.

"I'm sorry, I'm sorry," said Dalkin. "I'm so sorry."

The two Kurds sat uncomfortably. A short, mous-
tached waiter broke the silence.

"Would you care for an aperitif?"

Dalkin, ashen, was first to respond. "A large whiskey." He hoped alcohol would help.

"Water,'" said Matsalah.

In a show of Islamic solidarity, Faud ordered an
orange juice and Perrier.

Matsalah glared at Dalkin. This was just the kind
of attention he did not desire. Who knew, somebody
might even call the police?

"So," Dalkin picked it up like nothing had happened. "We are partners. Blow me. I mean, sorry.
Crinkum crankum, pop-a-nut."

Faud shifted uncomfortably, no longer sure of
this deal, which he had not yet mentioned to Matsalah.

"We shall see," said Faud. "We still await payment."

"And if it doesn't come this time?"

Faud winked. "There will be a next time. Payment will come."

The waiter, eyeing Dalkin nervously, set drinks
from his tray in front of the threesome.

Dalkin raised his glass. "To Kurdistan."

The two Kurds lifted their glasses and toasted.

Dalkin drained his whiskey in one gulp and

thumped his glass down. "Fuck-fuck-fuck-fuck-fuck-fuck-fuck-fuck-fuck-fuck-fuck-fuck! FUCK-SHIT-CUNT! COCKSUCKING CAMEL COPULATING KURDISH CUNTS!"

The Kurds shriveled in their seats.

"Oh, shit." Dalkin jerked his head. "Shit-shit-shit! Crinkum-crankum. Pop-a-nut! Goddamit! I'm going outside for some air!"

Faud and Matsalah nodded vigorously, relieved by this suggestion.

Dalkin stood up straight and smiled to himself as he strolled out of the back dining room, into the front dining room, all eyes fixed upon him. Tourette's did come in handy once in a while; the last outburst, his own creation. He heard whispers around him. ("Is that Bruce Willis?" "Must be." "What's he swearing about?")

Dalkin didn't stop strolling until he was outside, breathing the cool fresh air of Lake Lemann.

Faud's two bodyguards, sitting in their stretch Mercedes, stirred.

Dalkin stopped, took a deep breath, and scanned the surrounding area for a commercial van. There it was—parked around the bend. Dalkin walked the other direction, past the bodyguards. They watched him. The question was, would one or both get out and follow? The answer was: no. Their instructions were to stay put and protect their charge, period.

Dalkin beat a path around the corner, approaching the van from behind, out of the bodyguards' line of vision. He tapped lightly on the back door. It opened a crack.

"It's me. Bruce."

The door swung open and Dalkin climbed in. Tamara Burnham was inside with three young men clad in bluejeans, windbreakers and sneakers.

"You have my money?" asked Dalkin.

One of the men opened a large bag filled with rubber-banded stacks of hundred dollar bills.

"You're not going to take it back in there with you?" asked Tamara.

"No. Just checking. Hold onto it for me. I should charge you double."

"Why?"

"It's going to be a twosome—can you folks manage that?"

"Why two?"

"I've got Faud's partner here." Dalkin grinned. "Does the name Ahmed Matsalah mean anything to you?"

Tamara whistled softly. "Holy shit!"

"He's about as holy as the devil on Halloween. Are you ready for the bodyguards?"

"How many?"

"Two."

"Let's do it."

Dalkin backed out of the van, stepped into the shadows, and resumed his stroll. The two Kurds inside the car stirred as Dalkin reappeared. Dalkin walked to the car and tapped on the driver's side window. Unsmiling, the bodyguard looked up and allowed his window down three inches.

"Do you speak English?" asked Dalkin. "Crinkum crankum, pop-a-nut."

"A little," the puzzled driver grunted.

"I noticed something unusual down there." Dalkin pointed down the road, toward the van.

The two men looked behind them, then at each other, and shrugged. They said nothing, and did not seem inclined to do anything.

"That's all right," said Dalkin. "I'll mention it to Faud."

The passenger door popped open and a bodyguard climbed out. He walked down the block, peered into the front window of the van, then disappeared behind it. After that, nothing. Five minutes passed. The bodyguard who had remained behind the wheel shifted nervously and grumbled to himself in Arabic.

"Strange," Dalkin offered.

The driver got out, peered down the road, then turned toward Le Cheval Blanc.

"Aren't you going to look for him?" asked Dalkin.

"I tell Mr. Hamadi."

"No, wait!"

The bodyguard turned and was met by Dalkin head first, a butt to the forehead that landed him on his rump, seeing stars. Dalkin reached under the bodyguard's jacket and relieved him of his Makarov pistol.

"Get up," Dalkin commanded.

The driver stood, disoriented, rubbing his head, glaring at Dalkin.

"One word and you're dead," hissed Dalkin. "Start walking—that way!"

A reception committee at the van dealt with the second bodyguard as they had the first, binding and gagging him. The two men quietly prayed to Allah— to protect them from Faud Hamadi's wrath.

Dalkin returned to the Mercedes. He opened the door, reached inside and removed the keys from the ignition switch. Then he sauntered back into Le Cheval Blanc.

Faud and Matsalah were absorbed in rapid fire conversation, in Arabic, peppered with the English word Concorde.

"You're going to a hijack a Concorde?" asked Dalkin, sitting down.

"Shhhh! Shhhhhh!" Faud was mortified.

Matsalah flashed Dalkin a mean look.

"Well," Dalkin continued. "Just make sure Henry kiss-kiss-Kissinger is on board. Know what I mean? Kiss ass, kiss ass, speck and sauerkraut. Nems."

"You must be more discreet," growled Faud. "This is serious business."

"Of course," said Dalkin. "Of course, of course. Of course."

Matsalah shook his head in disgust. Who was this creep, and why did he know so much?

"You go right ahead and talk in Kurdish or Arabic or dohunkey or whatever you call it," said Dalkin. "I'll just order another whiskey."

The two Arabs remained silent. A waiter appeared to recite the day's specials. Faud and Matsalah ordered *tete de veau*—calves' head; Dalkin, *saumon frais* with ravioli in a *pistou* sauce with basilic, and another whiskey.

Dalkin pierced the vacuum of silence left in the waiter's wake. "Maybe I can help with your next job," he offered. "I always wanted to fly Concorde."

Going through Faud's mind was this: Why would Henry Kissinger hire this geek?

"You won't want to fly *this* Concorde," said Faud. "Unless you like to fall from 60,000 feet without parachute. Eh, Ahmed?" Faud nudged Matsalah, provoking a smile that revealed cracked, tobacco-stained teeth.

"No," said Dalkin. "Bungee jumping is as far as I go." He paused, then looked at Matsalah, a long thoughtful gape. "Ahmed, would it be presumptuous of me to ask if you were on the French Riviera this morning?"

Matsalah looked down, said nothing, grimaced.

"But why children?" Dalkin pressed. Though nobody had ordered it, Dalkin felt like dishing out some speck and sauerkraut. He'd already neutered the bodyguards. If these turds took radical exception to his style, he'd pull out the Makarov and blow their brains out—*tete de Kurd*—then drive the Mercedes to Evian in nearby France and disappear.

"Why *not* children?" Faud answered for Matsalah. "Our children die every day—in appalling conditions. And when they live, they live like dogs on so-called 'humanitarian aid.' Nobody cares. Not even CNN comes to see us."

Matsalah looked this way and that, uncomfortable, tensed.

Dalkin nodded at Faud, but focused his gaze on Matsalah. "Do you feel that slaughtering 28 innocent children is an act of bravery?" He felt Tourette's building. Without making the slightest effort to stop himself, Dalkin threw his head back, cracked his neck, then thrust it over the table toward Matsalah. "YOU COCKSUCKING CUNT-FACED PILE OF SHIT, PISS AND PUKE AND . . ."

Matsalah rose, flushed, angry. He threw his linen serviette at the table and stalked off.

". . . BUTT-BUGGERING BASTARD FROM HELL!"

Faud, too, had had quite enough. He glared at Dalkin, then pushed the table away and stood up.

"I'm sorry!" yelled Dalkin. "I can't help it!"

Dalkin's protests fell on deaf ears. Faud followed Matsalah, and Dalkin trailed them both.

"Does this mean our deal is off?" wailed Dalkin,

clicking at Faud's heels. "Fuck-fuck-fuck-fuck-fuck-fuck-fuck-fuck-fuck-fuck-fuck-fuck! FUCK! SHIT! GODDAMMIT! SHIT, SHIT, SHIT!"

There wasn't another sound in Le Cheval Blanc as Matsalah and Faud quickened their pace and Dalkin cursed uncontrollably, coming up from behind. Faud stopped to throw a wad of Swiss francs at the maitre d', who gladly accepted overpayment, and even more gladly held the door open.

Outside on the pavement, Matsalah led the charge to the Mercedes limo and put his hand on the back-door handle.

"Wait!" Faud froze, noticing the absence of body-guards.

"Gentlemen," said Dalkin, slowly, deliberately, with a crooked Bruce Willis smile gracing his coun-tenance. The two Kurds turned and faced Dalkin 15 feet away. Dalkin pointed a Makarov at them. "Gentle-men," he repeated. "This way please."

"Run!" yelled Faud.

The two men sprinted in different directions down the street.

The back doors of the van flew open and three CIA officers jumped out in pursuit.

Bernie Hewitt perused a legal document and looked up at his office clock: 3:30. He picked up the phone and touch-keyed a number. Jack Hudson answered.

"I'm going to file a brief this afternoon at the courthouse," said Hewitt.

"Maybe we should give them more time to negotiate?" said Hudson.

"No, no, no. This will *force* them to negotiate. They'll know we mean business."

"Why not just *call* the FBI director and *tell* him about the brief," suggested Hudson. "Give him a chance to . . ."

"I already know." Bryant Westgate cut in.

"You're eavesdropping on us!" Hewitt shouted. "You're tapping our phones! You'd better have a court order!"

"I'm sick of your legal bullshit," yelled Westgate. "Get the hell off this page—we're at a critical juncture!"

"No way," said Hewitt. "This book is about us from now on. We've had enough of you bossing us around, even if you are the director of the FBI. Either pay up or *you* get off this page—and see us in court—in *this* book."

"We'll see about that." Westgate clicked off.

"You see?"—Hewitt to Hudson—"now we're getting somewhere."

"I don't know." Hudson was shaken. "First that business with the IRS, now this—it's getting too crazy for me. Maybe we should take his offer and split. I don't like the limelight anyway."

The two men heard a double-click on their line.

"Who's there?" said Hewitt.

"I have the writer on a conference call," said Westgate.

"Good," said Hewitt. "Let's settle this right here and now."

"Gentlemen," I began. "I can't have you wrangling like this in my book."

"It's the FBI's fault," whined Hewitt. "We had a perfectly good story line—without all this malarkey—and he's wanted us written out ever since."

"But my story line is *better*," protested Westgate. "And it was *first*. You are a usurper!"

"And you're just jealous," said Hewitt. "Anyway, I'm not talking to you, I'm talking to the writer. Are you still there?"

"Yes," I replied.

"You must have had at least a subconscious reason for putting us in," said Hewitt.

"Okay, here's the truth." I was a tad sheepish. "I thought maybe Hudson's story would intertwine with yours. I didn't realize you two would be like oil and water. It hasn't worked. Sorry. If you can't come to terms I'm going to dump this whole thing and start a new story."

"Fine by me," said Hudson. "You think I like being raided by the IRS and handcuffed in front of my kids?"

"It was my idea to offer you $25,000, I said. "I'd like to see you fairly compensated for that."

"And then that's it?" snapped Hewitt. "The end of the line for us? And I'd bet we don't even get the next book, right?"

"Sort of. You're spent. But listen, Hewitt, you're just incidental anyway. Hudson was the main character. He could have gone to any lawyer—they're a dime a dozen."

"Two hundred and fifty thousand," said Hewitt, his feelings hurt. "It's easy—just type an extra zero."

"It's the principle," I said. "You're being greedy."

"Then we'll stay," said Hewitt.

"That's not a healthy attitude," I laughed. "I can simply *write* you out."

"Here, here," Westgate applauded. "Finally."

"Oh, yeah?" said Hewitt. "I'm calling *60 Minutes*."

13

Three CIA men hauled ass after Faud Hadi Hamade, who was half running, half stumbling down the street, cursing in Arabic. It was left to Jeff Dalkin to pursue Ahmed Matsalah, sprinting the other way into the night.

Matsalah was fast, but Dalkin brought the swarthy young Kurd down with a flying tackle. They tumbled into the street, fists flying, teeth grating. Matsalah was muscular, but Dalkin derived superior strength from sheer fortitude—from 28 innocent children. They were still at it, tearing at each other— Matsalah, biting and spitting—when two of the CIA contingent arrived. They moved quickly to untangle the two men from each other. One officer thrust a syringe into Matsalah's neck and squeezed. Fifteen seconds later, the Kurd was tranquilized into unconsciousness.

"Did you get Faud?" Dalkin brushed dirt and grit from his suit.

The men grunted. Dalkin followed them back to the van and peered inside as they laid Matsalah out flat. Faud was laying in a far corner, still conscious, bound and gagged, making piggie sounds.

Tamara Burnham leapt around Matsalah to greet Dalkin—and to block his entry.

"Change of plan, Bruce," she said. "You're not coming with us."

"But, but it was my plan!" Dalkin was stunned.

"We refined it. Sorry. Orders from headquarters. Bye!"

"What about my money?"

Tamara closed the double-doors and bolted them from inside as the van screeched off.

Dalkin stood alone in the street. "Fuck-fuck-fuck-fuck-fuck-fuck-fuck-fuck-fuck-fuck-fuck-fuck! FUCK! SHIT! SONOFABITCH! GODDAM FUCKING WHORE!"

This wasn't Tourette's. Dalkin meant every word.

Dalkin put his hand in his pants pocket. Yes! He had the key to Faud's Mercedes. He limped over, climbed behind the wheel, ignited, and tooled after the van—now fading from view, lights out. As he accelerated, Dalkin fingered Faud's mobile telephone. He listened as it clicked several times, connecting with a satellite high above.

"Thompson."

"Jim? Dalkin here. Slight problem."

"What is it?"

"My plan backfired."

"Backfired?"

"The spooks took off with our suspects. They tricked me. Cunt-farts."

"Where are they? Where are *you*?"

"In pursuit. On the road, heading for downtown Geneva."

"Don't lose them! Let me get this straight. They have Faud?"

"Correct. And Matsalah."

"Holy Catfish! How did they get *him*?"

"He was with Faud. A surprise dinner guest."

"I can't believe it. They have them both?"

"Correct."

"Fuck! Shit!"

"Yeah, I know," said Dalkin. "That's what I've been saying. I'm on their tail. What do you want me to do?"

"What *can* you do?"

"I'm working on pure adrenalin. I was kind of hoping *you'd* have some ideas."

"I'll phone the director. You stick with them."

"Got it."

"What's your number?" asked Thompson.

"I don't know—it's Faud's cell phone."

"Okay. Call me back in ten minutes."

Jim Thompson bounded into Bryant Westgate's office and broke the news.

"They *used* our agent!" Westgate exploded.

"Well, we were going to use *their* agents," Thompson reminded the director.

"I knew we shouldn't have assigned Jeff Dalkin," Westgate fumed.

"Dalkin captured Faud and Matsalah, didn't he?"

"Yeah—but he handed them to CIA on a silver platter. Carlton fucking Price will take all the credit and the president will have my balls! No, the president will have my scalp—*Henry Kissinger* will have my balls."

"It's not over yet. Dalkin's tailing them, awaiting further orders. Do you want him to get the Kurds back?"

"Can he?"

"If you say 'go,' he'll *try*."

Westgate thought a moment. "Yes. Do it."

The Director's intercom buzzed. It was Cheryl, with an urgent call for Jim Thompson.

"It's me," said Dalkin to Thompson. "What's the word?"

"If you think you can retrieve those Kurds, the word is go. Just don't kill anyone. And take it out of Switzerland, for chrissakes."

"Don't worry—that's where we're headed."

Dalkin's pursuit of the commercial van had taken him to the other side of Geneva, on a trunk road leading to Switzerland's Swiss border with France. The van traveled at a modest speed, so as not to attract attention, and Dalkin remained a respectable distance behind.

Swiss border guards waved both vehicles through, and the officers at the nearby French station did the same. At a fork, the commercial van chose the auto-route to Lyon.

With a half-tank of gas, Dalkin bided his time, reasoning that the CIA destination was either Paris—and the U.S. Embassy—or more likely Marseilles, which had a sleepy U.S. Consulate *and* access to the sea.

An hour later, past midnight, the van circled Lyon and pointed south. Marseilles. Fifteen minutes later the van veered right, into a rest stop offering food and gas.

Dalkin slowed and turned off his lights before exiting the autoroute. He cruised to a gradual stop 100 yards behind the van. He pocketed the Nokia phone and shoved the Makarov into his belt.

Dalkin climbed out silently. He did not close the door behind him, but left it slightly ajar to eliminate noise. Light-footed, he ambled toward the van. Slowly, deliberately, he put his left hand around the back door handle and turned gently. His right hand held the Makarov as he yanked the doors wide open.

"Hey!" blurted a male voice, just inside the van.

Dalkin shoved the Makarov, barrel down, into the man's lap. "Get out!" he hissed.

"What?"

"Get out or I'll blow your balls off!"

"Okay, okay." The agent slithered out of the van.

"What's going on back there?" Tamara Burnham called into the darkness from the front passenger seat.

Dalkin climbed in, swiftly closing the doors and bolting them.

Around him, four Kurds lay bound and gagged. Dalkin stepped over them, carelessly digging his heel into Matsalah's face; he hopped into the driver's seat next to Tamara.

"What the . . .?" Tamara was confused.

"Hello, Claudia," said Dalkin. "Nice to see you again. Crinkum-crankum, pop-a-nut." He pointed the Makarov at her with his left hand and turned the ignition key with his right. He hit the gas pedal as the other two agents alighted from the restaurant, their arms full of sandwiches and drinks and candy bars. Dalkin watched in his rearview mirror as they dropped everything to the ground and gave chase.

Burnham sat back, a wan smile on her face. "Very clever," she said. "I suppose you want your money?"

"Wrong. I want the cargo. But I'll take the money, too."

"You're digging yourself a very deep grave, Bruce. I would turn around and . . ."

"Hold this." Dalkin reached into his pocket and handed Tamara the Nokia. "Dial M, asterisk, then 202 . . ." Dalkin recited Jim Thompson's number.

"I get it," said Tamara. "Henry Kissinger wants to deliver these men himself?"

"Just dial," said Dalkin.

Burnham touch-keyed, listened for a ring, then handed the phone to Dalkin.

"Thompson," said a male voice.

"It's me. Dalkin. The payload is mine."

"Excellent! Where are you?"

"Outside of Lyon, heading south. Where do you want delivery."

There was no answer.

"Hello? Hello?" said Dalkin. "Hello?" He flung the phone over his shoulder. "Goddam battery's dead!"

"Now what, Bruce?"

Dalkin said nothing, deep in thought. And then his eye caught a flashing blue light in his rearview mirror. He looked at the speedometer—he'd been pushing 130 kilometers.

"Fuck-fuck-fuck-fuck-fuck-fuck-fuck-fuck-fuck-fuck-fuck-fuck! FUCK! SHIT! OH, SHIT!"

14

My phone rang. I picked it up in the middle of the fourth ring.

"Hello?"

"It's Bernie Hewitt."

"How the hell did you get my number?" I wasn't in the mood for this.

"The phone book."

"Bullshit. I'm not listed."

"All right. I asked my legal investigator to . . ."

"That's an invasion of privacy, Hewitt. You're a lawyer—you should know that."

"I just want to know, I *need* to know," said Hewitt, "is that it?"

"Is that *what*?"

"You're just going to forget about my client and me?"

"Apparently not," I said. "You called me, I answered, and—*voila!*—here you are again."

"Uh, yes, here I am. Where do we go from here?"

"Where would you *like* to go?"

"Give me a chance to turn this book around," Hewitt pitched, "to make it a gripping read. An intense courtroom drama. I sue the US government, make a case for taxpayers throughout the country—really stick it to the Feds, the IRS."

"I see. I assume I'm supposed to let you win, too?"

"All I'm asking is the chance to make my case in court. Let the judge decide."

"How magnanimous of you. I'd like to oblige, Bernie, but legal thrillers are passe."

"So is Middle Eastern terrorism. Vastly overdone."

I was unmoved.

"And look what the IRS did to my client," Hewitt added.

"I'm intimately familiar with what happened," I said. "But you are missing an important point: Jack Hudson would have been delighted with a 25 grand payoff. That's more money than he's ever had. This is about *you*. Admit it."

"Okay, okay—it's about me. Is that such a crime? I work in this shitty office in West Long Branch, New Jersey defending petty criminals and DWIs. This is my big chance. An important case. A book! Why, I could run for congress if this pans out. It's not fair. You're bailing me like a sack of potatoes because the FBI Director tells you to. *He's* the one who deserves to be dumped, not me."

"Be realistic," I said. "All your story has is the IRS treating your client unfairly. The IRS treats a *lot* of people unfairly. No court is going to award your client more than I've already offered. But Westgate's story has three horrifying terrorist attacks, the FBI and CIA engaged in professional rivalry, a lead character with Tourette's syndrome who looks like Bruce Willis, and a female character who looks like Claudia Schiffer and offers good potential for steamy gratuitous sex. You don't have *any* female characters."

"The IRS legal defense team could be headed by a female lawyer who looks like Meg Ryan—and I could do a sex scene with her."

"Unethical and you know it."

"Of course! That's what will make it a great story!"

"I'm sorry, Hewitt. You're wasting my ink." I was writing the old-fashioned way, with a pen and a tablet-sized notebook.

"All right, if that's your stance, I'll file suit against *you*." Hewitt was turning nasty.

"For what?"

"Violating my civil rights."

"Don't make me laugh. You're a white Anglo-Saxon. You don't have any civil rights. And, besides, you're just a figment of my imagination."

"Imagination is very potent," said Hewitt. "I'll file at night, while you're sleeping. You'll *dream* it."

"Bug off." I put the phone down.

Jeff Dalkin accelerated down the *autoroute*, pursued by the French cops.

"Aren't you going to stop?" Tamara Burnham smiled.

"Stopping is a no-win situation. They'll look inside the van and find our turds. Best case scenario, they'll get the collar themselves, make a secret deal and set them free in a week or two. Fart-faced frogs! Worst case, they'll throw us in jail for kidnapping."

"Not we," said Tamara. "*You*, baby. I'm one of the kidnapped."

"Like hell you are. These turds were mine. You kidnapped them from *me*."

"That's illogical."

"I don't care. Now they're mine again. You can get out any time you want. I'll even let you keep the bodyguards."

The French police car, more powerful than Dalkin's commercial van, was closing in.

"Shit, shit, shit!" Dalkin pounded the steering wheel. "I guess we'll have to stop. We'll have to take them, too."

"Oh, no," said Tamara. "What would we *do* with them?"

"I don't know. You're CIA. Cunt-farts. Brainwash them or something."

"Get serious."

"Okay—what do *you* suggest?"

"Let me handle it. I'll tell them I, Claudia Schiffer,

and you, Bruce Willis, are having a secret love affair and we're speeding to stay one step ahead of the tabloids. They'll probably just want our autographs."

"Okay. But if you screw up, Plan B cuts in."

"What's Plan B?"

"I don't know yet." Dalkin removed his foot from the gas pedal and veered onto the shoulder. He slowed and stopped. The police car followed, braking to a halt 50 yards behind the van. The French officers remained in their vehicle for several minutes.

"What are they up to?" said Dalkin.

"Checking out the tags probably," said Tamara.

"Where did you rent this van from?"

"We didn't rent it—we borrowed it."

"From who?"

"A parking lot."

"Fuck-fuck-fuck-fuck-fuck-fuck-fuck-fuck-fuck-fuck-fuck-fuck! FUCK! SHIT! Oh, SHIT! GOD-DAMIT!"

Dalkin watched in his rearview mirror as the police officers climbed out walked cautiously toward him. When they were four-fifths of the way up, Dalkin hit the gas pedal and burned rubber onto the *autoroute*. The officers scrambled back to their car. Driving without lights, Dalkin sped down the motorway, looking for an edge. He rounded a bend and whizzed into a quiet rest stop. The police car sped by, its siren wailing.

"Now what?" said Tamara. "French police everywhere will be looking for us."

"We need another vehicle," said Dalkin.

"Gee, what did you get your college degree in, The Obvious?"

"This is *your* fault," said Dalkin. "I told you to *rent* a van, not steal one. Can't you people at CIA—cunt-farts—do anything without breaking the law?"

"We don't like things traced back to us."

Dalkin scratched his head. "Is there anyone you can call—your station chief? A duty officer?"

"Why don't you call Henry Kissinger?"

"I don't work for kiss ass, kiss ass, speck and sauerkraut. Goddamit! I mean kiss-kiss-kiss . . . kiss ass, kiss ass, speck and sauerkraut-nems. Oh, fuck it!"

"No? Then who?"

"The Bureau."

"WHAT?"

"You know *what*—the FBI."

"You mean we're on the same side?" Tamara Burnham sat dumbfounded, her dainty Claudia Schiffer-like jaw dropping into her lap.

"I'm FBI. You're CIA. Cunt-farts. That *ain't* the same side—and you know it. Pop-a-nut."

"I want my money back," said Tamara.

"Nope. It belongs to the Bureau now."

"But you tricked me!"

"So what. You spooks at CIA—cunt-farts—are always tricking people."

"Uh-oh," said Tamara. "We have somebody else on our tail now."

Dalkin peered into his mirror and did a double-take. A white BMW was closing in. "I think I know who it is."

"You do? Who?"

"This is great! You'll see." Dalkin eased the pressure of his foot on the gas pedal and slowed, allowing the BMW to pull up alongside on the left.

"They're taking pictures of us!" shouted Tamara, covering her hands with her face.

"Of course they are! Don't worry."

Dalkin rolled down his window. The photographer, surprised, rolled down his own.

"Jeez, you found me." Dalkin smiled his crooked smile. "We might as well give you the whole story—and then you'll leave us alone, right? Dirty bottoms."

"Of course, mate!" The photographer turned and spoke with the driver, who beamed, already calculating the astronomical bonus he expected to receive for landing this splash exclusive—and now an interview, too! The Gods were obviously looking down upon their nocturnal muckraking.

"Next rest stop," shouted Dalkin.

Six kilometers later, Dalkin pulled off the road, into a deserted rest stop. The BMW followed. Its two doors flung open and the reporter and his photographer climbed out, smiling, proud of themselves.

Dalkin pocketed his van's ignition key, stepped out and confronted the two tabloid reporters with his Makarov.

"What the . . ." The reporter raised his hands.

The photographer raised his camera.

"Drop it," demanded Dalkin. "No pictures."

"Is this some kind of joke?" said the reporter. "You can't do this to us!"

Dalkin didn't answer.

"Take a picture," the reporter commanded his photographer. "It's just a toy gun."

The lensman raised his camera again.

Dalkin pointed his weapon. "I'm warning you. Wanking wieners."

The photographer snapped and flashed. Dalkin fired. BOOM! The single shot sounded like a bomb in the eerily quiet night.

The camera fell to the ground, smashing on impact. The lensman felt himself around his torso for a wound. Nothing. He gaped at Dalkin, whose pistol was pointed at the sky.

"That's better," said Dalkin.

"You, you, you can't do this to us, Bruce," stammered the reporter. "That's assault with a deadly weapon."

"I don't give a pig's butt. I'm sick and tired of you sleaze-balls making my life a misery. I think I'll bury you in that field." Dalkin waved his Makarov at the grassy hills.

"But, but we're just doing our job!"

"Is that what you call it? It's your job to follow me around 24 hours a day and write lies about every

15

My phone rang. I thought it was Bernie Hewitt again.

"No, it's me," said Westgate. "I don't like where this scenario is headed. How could anyone in their right mind, especially someone as beautiful as Claudia, be turned on by Tourette's?"

"You mean you would have preferred if Claudia took off with the Kurds and left Bruce in the middle of nowheresville?"

"I didn't say that."

"I'll decide what you say and don't say. You're just jealous, Rodney."

"Don't call me Rodney!"

"Don't call *me*, period. How am I supposed to write with you and Bernie Hewitt constantly interrupting me?"

"Is *he* still around?"

"He wants to be. He says he's going to *sue* me."

"Be careful. Anyone can sue anyone for anything in this country."

"But he's my own creation."

"I realize that. Why don't you just have what's-his-name—Hudson—fire him?"

"I don't want to get into that right now—I'm having too much fun with Bruce and Claudia."

"Meanwhile, I just sit here at my desk, waiting," whined Westgate. "I never leave my friggin' office . . . hold on, I have another call."

I waited. Westgate returned to me 30 seconds later.

"That was Hewitt!" he hollered.

"Better you than I."

"He says he's going to sue *me*, too!"

"For what?"

"He didn't say. You must do something."

"*You* do something. This is all your fault."

"*My* fault?"

"Don't act all innocent with me. It was you who first tried to interfere with what I'm writing—and now Hewitt thinks he can do the same. See what you started?"

"Do something!"

"Okay. I'm taking my phone off the hook. See you, bye."

It was about two a.m. when Dalkin and Tamara roared out of France in their BMW. Tamara, still behind the wheel, cruised into a 24-hour service station as Dalkin dozed in the seat next to her. He awakened when the car stopped.

"Huh? Where are we?"

"Germany," said Tamara. "I'm going to fill the tank."

Dalkin turned to check on his captives. They were asleep.

"P-U." Dalkin held his nose. "I'm going to make a call."

"Wait," said Tamara. "Let's agree on something. We *both* take credit—a liaison, right?"

"Right. A liaison. It has a nice ring to it."

Dalkin trudged off and purchased a German phone card from the cashier. He slid it into a phone and touch-keyed Jim Thompson's number, checking his watch: just past eight p.m. in Washington.

"Thompson."

"It's Dalkin."

"What's going on?" Thompson had been sitting on the edge of his desk awaiting this call.

"We're in Germany."

"Who's *we*?"

"Me, the two turds—and Tamara, the spook-stress."

"What is *she* doing with you?"

"We're partners. Crinkum-crankum, pop-a-nut."

"What?"

"It was the only way."

"The director isn't going to like this."

"I don't like this, either. The Kurds have shit and pissed themselves. They're stinking up my car. Uh, not my car—does the director know anyone at the *National Enquirer*?"

"I don't know. Why?"

"He may have to call them and sort out a little problem."

"What problem?"

"We borrowed a car from two of their reporters."

"Why?"

"Who, what, where, when, why and how," said Dalkin. "Pecksniff!"

"What?"

"Exactly."

"Exactly what?"

"Exactly this, goddamit: Tell me where you want these fucking turds!"

"Okay, okay—calm down. I'm going to find the director."

Dalkin stood by watching Tamara pump gas.

"The director says no." Thompson was back on line with Dalkin.

"No, what?"

"No to partnering with the Agency."

"I'm already *doing* it," said Dalkin. "Speck and sauerkraut, nems."

"The director says he may be able to *un*do that."

"What the hell are you talking about?"

"He knows the writer."

"The who?"

"The writer of this book. He says he's going to talk to him about it."

"Are you all crazy over there?" hollered Dalkin. "Since when do characters in a book talk to the author? I *like* the way things are going! Crinkum-crankum, pop-a nut!"

"Hold on." Thompson pressed the blinking inter-com button. "Yes, Bryant?"

"I can't get through to the author," said Westgate. "I think his phone is off the hook."

"What do you want me to tell Dalkin," said Thompson. "He's holding."

"Order Dalkin to Frankfurt. Wake up our legat in Germany—order them to Frankfurt, too. Then call the Air Force. Order up transportation from Germany. And organize a press conference for me at nine tomor-row morning."

"Got it." Thompson returned to Dalkin. "Drive to Frankfurt, Dalkin. Phone me when you reach the outskirts and I'll give you more specific instructions."

An hour later, Westgate tried calling me again. I had re-plugged my phone in anticipation. After all, if I was going to start hiding from my own characters, I might as well put down my pen and become a clerk at Rite Aid.

"You answered," said Westgate.

"Observant, aren't we?"

"No need for sarcasm. I'm just calling to thank you."

"For what?"

"Things are working out my way." Westgate was smug. Too smug.

"It's all spontaneity," I said. "I told you before, there's no plan, no outline. I just make it up as I go along. Even *I* don't know what's going to happen until after my first cup of coffee."

"I'll just put a suggestion in your ear, then I'll leave you alone to write."

"That's good of you."

"I will personally meet Dalkin and Tamara Burnham to congratulate them on their success. I ask Tamara out to dinner. She accepts. We drive to the Inn at Little Washington, you know, an hour into the Virginia countryside? One thing leads to another. After a four course meal with lots of expensive wine we take a room. And *you* get your gratuitous sex scene!"

Westgate spoke like he was doing me a favor.

"No need," I said. "It's already happening."

"What is?"

"The sex stuff. Tamara is blowing Dalkin at 160 kilometers an hour."

"What?"

"On the *autobahn*—heading west."

"Impossible," snapped Westgate. "They're driving to Frankfurt. That's east."

"Sorry, Bryant. I guess things aren't working out as well as you thought they were. Gotta go." I put down the phone and unplugged it again.

"Fuck-fuck-fuck-fuck-fuck-fuck-fuck-fuck-fuck-fuck-fuck-fuck! FUCK! GOD! OH, GOD! OH...!"
Tamara Burnham's face was in Dalkin's lap, her mouth firmly planted around his dick.

"OH MY GOD!!"
Tamara bobbed up and down, massaging Dalkin's member with her tongue while the Kurds in back pricked their ears.

"HOLY FUCKING CHRIST!!"
Dalkin exploded.

Four thousand miles away, Bryant Westgate was also exploding.

"Cancel my press conference!" He was hollering at Jim Thompson. "They're *not* on their way to Frankfurt!"

"How do you know?" asked Thompson.

"I have an extremely reliable source," said Westgate. "They must be following Carlton Price's instructions, goddamit! I'm going to call that bastard!" Westgate picked up his phone and touch-keyed the CIA Director's personal number.

"Carlton Price."

"Aha—you're working late, too," said Westgate.

"We expect to bring an important covert operation to a conclusion tonight."

"Are you talking about the apprehension of Faud Hadi Hamade and Ahmed Matsalah?"

"Yes, as a matter of fact. But how do *you* know about it?"

"Me? It's my agent who apprehended them!"

"Tut, tut. It is a career operations officer of ours stationed in Switzerland."

"You know who I'm talking about," Westgate seethed. "Dalkin. Jeff Dalkin."

"Oh? The Kissinger Associate with Tourette's?"

"He's not a Kissinger Associate. He's *our* agent."

"Whomever he really works for hardly matters now. *We* are bringing in Hamade and Matsalah."

"Like hell you are!"

"We'll see. Have a nice evening, Bryant. And give Cheryl one for me, would you?"

"WHAT?"

But Price was gone.

"Do you have any aspirin?" This was Ahmed Matsalah, from the floor of the backseat. He had managed to remove his gag.

"What for?" Dalkin was running on caffeine. It was three a.m. and dawn was already breaking.

"Headache."

"Twenty-eight sets of parents are waking up this morning to bury their children and I'm supposed to give you aspirin for a fucking headache? Fuck you, you fucked up fucking Kurdish cunt! And shut up! Speck and sauerkraut! Nems. Not another noise out of either of you scumbags or I'll turn you into road-kill!"

Dalkin had rolled down his window and opened the sun roof, but he couldn't eradicate the stench from the backseat.

"If it were up to me," continued Dalkin, "you filthy bastards would never leave this car—you'd keep pissing and shitting until you suffocated from your own poisonous vapors."

"We're here," said Tamara, after re-gagging Hamade. "Stop at the next gas station."

Dalkin braked and veered into the service area. He parked a discreet distance from the office, alighted from the car and found a phone.

A minute later he connected. "I'm here," said Dalkin.

"What?"

"I'm here," Dalkin repeated. "In Frankfurt. You said to call for specific instructions. So, give them to me."

"But . . . ?" Jim Thompson was confused. "We thought . . . you're in Frankfurt?"

"Affirmative. Isn't that where you said to go?"

"Hold on." Thompson buzzed Westgate. "Dalkin's on line from Frankfurt. So much for your reliable source."

"You got Dalkin? Put me on!" The line clicked.

"Hello, hello?" said Dalkin.

"This is Director Westgate. Where are you?"

"Outskirts of Frankfurt," said Dalkin. "As ordered."

"Who is in charge?" demanded Westgate. "You or the Agency operative?"

"We're not engaged in an ego contest, sir. We're just trying our best to bring in two suspects."

"Did she blow you?"

"What?"

"Did she blow you—you know, give you a blow job?"

"With all due respect, sir, that's none of your fucking business!"

"Excuse me," said Westgate, "but it ties into something else I heard."

"I'm sorry, sir. If I seem short it's because I've been up almost 24 hours, I've been jerked around by almost everyone, and I'm with two Kurds who've been pissing and shitting themselves all night. I just want to know one thing: where do you want them?"

"Jim." Westgate addressed Thompson. "Have you alerted the legat?"

"Yes, Bryant."

"And they are on their way to the airport?"

"Yes. ETA four a.m."

"You got that, Dalkin?"

"Four a.m.," echoed Dalkin. "Where at the airport?"

"They'll be in a green van, unmarked," said Thompson. "At four a.m. precisely they will stop at the drop-off area in front of the main terminal. Flash your lights once to signal them, then follow. They will lead you to a deserted area for a transfer."

"Got it. Will there be a representative of the Agency—cunt farts—on hand?"

"What does that have to do with *you?*" Westgate interjected.

"That's my deal with Tamara Burnham..."

"You're not authorized to make deals!" snapped Westgate. "This is a Bureau operation, from start to finish."

"Not any more, sir," said Dalkin. "It has become a joint operation."

"*You* presume to tell *me* what kind of operation this is?"

"Yes, sir. That's how it evolved. Pop-a-nut, nems."

"You're fired, Dalkin."

"Wait a minute..." Thompson interrupted.

"No, Jim, that's okay," said Dalkin. "Thank you, Mr. Westgate—I was hoping you'd say that. Anus-brained fart-bag."

"What? Why?"

"Because as a private international bounty hunter my fee is one million dollars for capturing and turning over international terrorists . . ."

"You can't . . ." Westgate began.

"If it's too much for your budget, sir, I'll try CIA—cunt-farts."

"This is blackmail!" hollered Westgate.

"No, sir. You fired me. This is how I earn a living. Crinkum-crankum, pop-a-nut."

"One million dollars?"

"One million for each terrorist. Two million total."

"Goddamit, Dalkin! I won't stand for this!"

"Sit down and think about it, sir. I'll phone back in ten minutes. After we talk to Mr. Price at CIA—cunt farts."

"No! Don't . . .!"

Dalkin replaced the phone and returned to the BMW to confer with Tamara. She climbed out, leaving Dalkin to guard the Kurds, and made her way to the phone. She inserted Dalkin's card and dialed Langley.

"CIA."

"Director Price, please."

Price answered himself. "Carlton Price."

"Mr. Price? This is Tamara Burnham. I apologize for not going through channels, but I'm at a critical juncture in a sensitive operation and it is the middle of the night here in Germany."

"Yes, Tamara. Please go on."

"Are you aware of the assistance given us by an associate of Henry Kissinger?"

"Yes."

"The FBI director has just offered him two million dollars to turn our suspects over to them."

"Who is in command of the suspects?" asked Price.

"Under the circumstances, we both are."

"Didn't this Kissinger Associate desert three of our operatives and try to hijack the suspects?"

"Yes. He is determined to benefit from this situation. The question is, can we top the FBI's offer?"

"Miss Burnham, is this chap Dalkin conducting an auction?"

"Yes, sir. He appears to be doing that."

"And is there no way you can neutralize him?"

"Not without jeopardizing the safe delivery of the suspects, sir."

"Then I shall be prepared to pay Mr. Dalkin 2.5 million for his services rendered, based on a conviction of the suspects—inclusive of the $75,000 he has already received. And on condition that this closes the deal and he does not try to gain a higher bid from the Bureau."

"Excellent, sir."

"What is your position?"

"We're outside of Frankfurt."

"Fine. I want you to drive to Wiesbaden. I'll

make arrangements for receiving your party. Phone
me when you arrive." Price recited his direct number.

Tamara returned to the BMW and conveyed the
news to Dalkin.

Faud Hadi Hamade made muffled noises from
the backseat.

"I think that piece of shit wants to say something," said Dalkin.

"You want me to take off his gag?" asked Tamara.

"Yeah, I could use a laugh."

Tamara leaned back and un-gagged Faud.

The Kurd choked. "It's nothing," he gasped. "I
give you *ten million* to set us free."

"Fuck you! Shut up!" shouted Dalkin. "You butt-
buggering bastards—you're gonna suck big black
baloneys where you're going."

Dalkin got out of the car and returned to the
phone to dial Thompson.

"Thompson."

"Hi, Jim. Tell the director my offer is withdrawn.
I'm working for the Agency—cunt farts."

"C'mon, Jeff—I brought you into this. My ass is
on the line."

"Westgate fired me—you heard him."

"But he . . ."

"Sorry, Jim—gotta go. Pop-a-nut."

Bryant Westgate was apoplectic with rage when
Thompson told him the news.

"Intercept them!" he hollered. "Get our legats on the road! Intercept!"

"How?"

"We know they're on the fringes of Frankfurt, right? They drove up from Lyon so they must be south or southwest. Get a chopper up looking for them! Get five choppers up there!"

"Then what?"

"Let's find them—then we'll decide."

My phone rang. I picked up.

"Let me guess," I said. "Bryant Westgate?"

"Very funny." Westgate sounded costive. "I need a word with you."

"Don't start with me," I said. "I thought maybe you had learned your lesson from Hewitt. But no, you're as tight as my father-in-law."

"How can you blame *me*? You're the one writing this stuff!"

"Yes and no. I give my characters a huge degree of latitude. How do you think you're able to call me?"

"But why did you tell me Dalkin was heading west?"

"Sorry. I got confused."

"YOU GOT CONFUSED? You're *not* supposed to get confused."

"It happens."

"Did Tamara really give Dalkin a blowjob?"

"Yeah. That part's true. But no point getting jealous. That was just a taster, so to speak. Look, don't bother sending up a helicopter. It's all over."

"What do you mean, all over?"

"You lost. Call it a day. Go home. Screw your wife—but *not* in this book. This has gone on long enough. I'm not getting involved in any cockamamie scheme to intercept Dalkin and Tamara and the Kurds."

"But you said I have latitude," Westgate protested. "Flexibility to do what I want?"

"You *had* latitude. Past tense. I'm reeling you in."

"But, but I'm supposed to beat Carlton Price. Otherwise you would have made *him* your lead character."

"No, I had no plan—total spontaneity—and I gave you every chance. You blew it. You're an example of over-realized potential. That pompous ass Price won naturally."

"There must be something you can do?"

"No. I'm out of ideas. Even two cappuccinos haven't stirred up anything. I want to move on."

"So this is it?"

"For the moment. Maybe I'll get back to you."

"What if you don't?" Westgate's voice trembled.

"Goodbye, Bryant."

16

"**O**h my God!" Tamara Burnham had positioned her pelvis at the foot of the king-size bed. Jeff Dalkin was kneeling within her spreadeagled legs, brushing her pussy with his tongue. "Yes! Yes! Yessssssssss!! Come! Come in, Bruce! NOW!"

Dalkin rose and slid his rigid dick into her swollen lips, watching it disappear into a mound of sand-colored pubic hair. "Ohhhhhhhhhh!'

Tamara gasped.

"Fuck-fuck-fuck-fuck-fuck-fuck-fuck-fuck! Oh, oh! Oh, God! I'm gonna give you a good fucking!" Dalkin pulled out. "This way."

Dalkin maneuvered Tamara to the center of the bed and lay on his back. Tamara tugged on his dick, pumping it, increasing the blood supply until his thing felt like a lead pipe. Then she climbed on top and lowered herself onto him, swallowing it with her pussy. She leaned over him, twisting and turning, brushing the nipples of her large, round tits against his lips.

Dalkin grabbed hold of Tamara's midsection and tumbled her onto her side, then her back. He shoved a pillow beneath her butt as she rested her long legs onto his shoulders. Dalkin thrust into her with all his soul, the two of them heaving, humping, moaning and wailing. The bedsprings squealed. The whole bed trembled.

"Oh! OHHHH! BALL ME, BRUCE!" shrieked Tamara.

"God. Oh, God! Oh, God . . . Claudia . . . AHHHHHHHHHHHH!"

And then all was quiet.

Dalkin rolled onto his back, caught his breath, dipped his head down to the floor and peeked under the valance.

"Are you two okay?"

The two Kurds lay beneath the bed, bound and gagged, praying quietly to Allah that they not be crushed to death.

Dalkin rose, showered, dressed; Tamara lingered, and finally picked up the phone and touch-keyed Carlton Price's direct line. It rang. He answered.

"It's Tamara. We're at a roadside inn outside of Wiesbaden."

"Fine, Tamara. Can you tell me *exactly* where?"

Tamara related the details, including the room number.

"The suspects are in the room?"

"Yes. We needed rest and we thought it prudent not to leave them in the car."

"Our team should arrive in 30 minutes. They will knock four times, pause, then once again."

"We'll be here. Sir, do you know anyone at the *National Enquirer?*"

17

One Week Later

New York Times: **CIA Captures Terrorist Suspects**

CIA Director Carlton Price announced today that his operations branch secretly apprehended two Kurdish men believed to be responsible for a recent spate of terrorist attacks in Washington, London and the South of France.

Sources in the intelligence community say that the suspects were captured in Europe several days ago, and that they were flown to the United States from Germany aboard a U.S. Navy jet.

The Kurds, named as Faud Hadi Hamade and Ahmed Matsalah, are being held in Quantico, Virginia as material witnesses. Indictments are expected within days.

Washington was stunned six weeks ago when a lone terrorist attacked Au Bon Pain, a coffee shop across the street from the J. Edgar Hoover Building . . .

Washington Post: FBI Director Resigns

Bryant Westgate, the FBI's director for six years, has tendered his resignation as America's top law enforcement officer. Mr. Westgate was thought to be under pressure since last month, when a terrorist attack took the lives of 14 FBI agents on his Bureau's doorstep.

The White House announced that the President has accepted the resignation "with regret and deep appreciation of Mr. Westgate's service to his country."

White House aides are said to be preparing a short-list of possible nominees to fill the gap left by Westgate . . .

National Enquirer: Bruce Willis and Claudia Schiffer In Love Tangle
by Newland Squillers

In a bizarre attempt to conceal their sizzling extramarital romance, superstar Bruce Willis and super-model Claudia Schiffer held me and my photographer at gunpoint in France last week.

Willis, who said he was acting on behalf of the Celebrity Liberation Front, pointed a loaded pistol at me while Claudia Schiffer tied rope around my wrists and ankles. She also tied a gag on my mouth.

The world-famous lovebirds left us on the roadside and made their getaway in our rented BMW . . .

World Weekly News: Character in Book Sues His Creator

New Jersey criminal lawyer Bernie Hewitt has a serious gripe. He believes that he and his client were unfairly "bumped" from a *book* that, he claims, should have been about their case against the IRS.

Now Bernie has filed suit in federal court in Trenton, New Jersey claiming $10,000,000 in punitive damages from the author who created him.

Part of Bernie's complaint is that the author used the FBI in an attempt to bribe him into silence.

"We're setting a legal precedent," Bernie announced at a press conference at the Long

Branch Hilton hotel. "It is high time that fictional characters in books take a stand against those who would manipulate them—and isolate them at will."

Reached at a bar in Monte Carlo, the author said, "I'm thinking up a proper counteraction."

Two Weeks Later

World Weekly News: Lawyer Bursts into Flames

In what is thought to be a rare case of Spontaneous Human Combustion, attorney Bernard Hewitt burst into flames while strolling the boardwalk in Long Branch, New Jersey . . .